D1481036

PRAIRIE PRINCESS

PRAIRIE PRINCESS

By

MARGARET EPP

Illustrations by

ROBERT G. DOARES

MOODY PRESS

CHICAGO

Contents

CHAPTER   **PAGE**

1. To Town on a Saturday 7

2. A Skeleton—and a Mystery 17

3. Safely Through Another Week 27

4. Sunday Company 36

5. Linda 46

6. The Magic Twenty-fifth 56

7. June Picnic 66

8. First of July 76

9. Summertime 85

10. Sarah's Rebellion 95

11. Aunt Jane 106

12. A Dream Come True 117

CHAPTER 1

To Town on a Saturday

SARAH NAOMI SCOTT was ten. And she had eleven freckles on her pert nose. And she could think of at least twelve reasons why she should be outdoors right this minute.

Instead, she hung over the sill of the upstairs window, teetering and wishing— What she ought to be doing was to collect all the lamps from all the rooms of the house. Eight lamps! Trimming the wicks, and filling the lamps with oil, and washing and rinsing and polishing the globes was Sarah's Saturday morning chore. And that was all right any other Saturday. But this was a Saturday morning *in spring*.

A wild and happy kind of morning. Warm wind tickled your face. Sunlight flashed on the puddles in the yard. You could hear the whirring clickety-clickety-click of the clipper as Father cut the shaggy winter hair off Daisy and Beauty, the chunky Percheron mares. And you could hear the mother hens clucking to their little fluffy babies. And you could hear the meadowlark singing,

"I—was—here—a—year—ago!"

"You were! Sure, you were!" shouted Sarah, and she pounded her fists on the sill. "I found your nest with the cute little eggs in it."

7

Father looked up from his job smiling. "Come on down, Princess," he called.

"I *can't*. I have to do the lamps!" wailed Sarah.

Stuart, who held the horses for Father, called encouragingly. "Do it quickly then, so you'll be free."

Stuart knew a lot. He went to high school in town five times a week, driving all the way in the buggy. He was smart. Only a few farm boys got to go to high school. But maybe he didn't know what it was like to have to clean lamps when there was so much to see in the yard.

Robbie had let the calves out of the barn now, and they were going wild, just plain silly wild. They galloped and pranced and kicked up their heels. They rushed around in circles and in figure eights. Their funny little tails stuck out at funny angles. They bawled, and Spencer barked and laughed, hanging out his tongue. Spencer was a handsome collie, so of course he had to have a very special name.

"Sarah Naomi Scott! What's happened to you?"

Sarah sighed. That was Kathleen, her big sister. She was terribly old. Almost twenty! And she was bossy sometimes. Like now.

"I want to use the kitchen table. Get a wiggle on!"

"Coming!"

Regretfully Sarah pulled her head back into the house. She took up Kathleen's lamp—the one with the flowery bowl and the flowery shade to match—and she carried it carefully down the stairs.

In the kitchen Mother was kneading the bread dough. Kathleen was washing the cupboards. There were piles and stacks of dishes and pots and pans to wash. But that was Kathleen's job.

Cleaning the lamps was an important chore too. Besides,

if Mother felt like it, she told stories about when *she* was a ten-year-old. Long ago. Almost thirty years ago. That was when she came to Saskatchewan from the East with her father and mother, riding in the train with many other settlers. Mother would rock back and forth as she punched the dough, and she would remember aloud how it was then.

Not this morning, though. She was in a hurry this morning.

"When are you leaving for town, Mother?" said Kathleen.

"Right after dinner."

"Ooooh! May I go too? Please, Mother, may I?" In her eagerness Sarah almost dropped the flowery shade.

"Careful there," warned Mother.

"But, please, mayn't I?"

"I don't know. You have all the boots to polish, remember."

"I'll do them when we get back."

"I can't promise to be home early enough for that, Sarah."

"I'll do them this morning. Right after the lamps."

Mother glanced at the clock. "If you manage without breaking a globe—well, we'll see."

We'll see was a bothersome answer. Sometimes it meant yes. Sometimes it meant no. And the bother was that you often didn't know until the very last minute if it meant yes or no.

Sarah hurried so that her hands shook. One lamp almost slipped from her grasp. Trimming the wicks was another bother. You had to shape the corners so the flame wouldn't blacken the glass. But when the last lamp was safely back in place, Sarah became a little whirlwind, dashing from room to room, scooping up the boots and shoes into her apron, a big bundle of them.

Polishing boots was one thing you could do outdoors, sitting in the sunshine on the porch. The green and yellow baby goslings in their pen nearby saw her and kept calling in their soft voices, "Peelee, peelee, peelee!" Spencer came trotting to lick at her bare legs and to sit back, waving his white tail and laughing. Ginger, the big cat, who was Spencer's special pal, came to rub her ankles. Everything and everybody was saying, "Come and play, come and play!"

But—not this morning, thank you!

"You see," she explained, "I'm going to town. At least, I *think* I am. Mother said *we'll see*. And I *think* that means yes today. *If* I get the boots cleaned and polished."

Some were muddy and had to be scraped and brushed first. Some were black and some were brown. She had to open two boxes of paste, and they were hard to open when you were in a tearing hurry. Then all of the Sunday shoes had to be rubbed and buffed till they shone. Sarah hurried, but she still had a pair left to do when Kathleen stuck her head out the door.

"Dinner's ready!" she called.

"Coming!" came Father's answering shout.

Oh, wowie! Hurry, hurry, hurry, Sarah!

Father and Stuart and Robbie came clumping up the walk.

"Well, look at our busy bootblack," said Stuart, pulling a bit of her hair as he passed.

Sarah didn't look up. Her hands with the brown and black smudges went flashing back and forth, rubbing, rubbing—

"Whoowee! I'm through!" she yelled triumphantly through the screen door then.

"About time," said Kathleen.

"You'll have to scrub your hands after prayer," said Mother. "Can't keep your father and the boys waiting. They have a busy day."

There was a Saturday kind of dinner. Soup, and baked dishes—all made of bits of leftovers. Sarah thought secretly that Father wouldn't mind very much waiting for that! But there was a baked apple dessert too, with lots of caramel sauce. The trouble was, in the Scott home you had to have a bowlful of soup and a good helping of the baked beans, ham, potatoes, creamed chicken and onions before you got to the dessert. Sarah had had a late start besides.

(Her hands were *almost* clean though.)   And she still didn't know if *we'll see* meant yes or no.

"Robbie could go with you, Mother," suggested Father. Sarah peered under her thick dark lashes at her twelve-year-old brother. His face was long and worried looking. Usually he liked going to town, of course. But this was spring—a Saturday in spring. Robbie had planned to go gopher-hunting with Spencer this afternoon. Sarah didn't need to ask. She was sure of it. You got five whole cents for every gopher tail!

The longer and sadder Robbie's face became the happier Sarah felt.

"The only horse available for the small buggy today is Hyacinthe," Father continued. "And she's a bit frisky this time of year. Not really broken to single harness."

"I think I can manage her," said Mother. "And I won't need Robbie's company. Sarah would like to go to town with me."

"She would, would she?" Father pulled her braid teasingly.

Her hair was funny like his own. Sometimes it looked dark, dark brown. Almost black. Other times it looked as if red flames must be burning deep inside.

After dinner Sarah put on her school dress and her second-best sandals. She thought it a nuisance to wear a sweater, but Mother said she must if she wished to go. So she wore it.

Sitting behind Hyacinthe was a little bit scary today. She had a bouncy way of running. Her ears kept twitching, and her eyes rolled. Sarah couldn't help thinking of the deep ravine that cut across the road about halfway from here to Blakely. It had a tricky slope.

They trotted past the Slocum place—and the Darnley farm. And Mother was right. Today's warm breeze didn't feel quite so warm when you were riding high in a buggy like this. But all the same Sarah left her sweater unbuttoned to show she really wasn't chilly at all! And they passed Aunt Jane Bolton's farm.

"A lot of bedding sunning on the line," remarked Mother.

"Maybe Aunt Jane is getting a married hired man again this spring," said Sarah. "And maybe this time there'll be a girl for me to play with."

The Darnleys had only boys. So did the Slocums. Next to Aunt Jane's place was the Heathe place. They had girls, but all of them were about as old as Kathleen! Sarah had no friend closer than Susan Gerrick, and *she* lived four and a half miles west of the Scotts.

Blakely was south and east of Sarah's home.

They were close to the ravine now. Sarah felt a funny crawly feeling—like a string pulling tight and tighter inside her. Hyacinthe was bouncing again. And now she snorted. And now she was heading straight down the steep slope, faster, faster, the buggy swaying. Mother's hand grew white as she held the reins.

"Behave yourself, Hyacinthe," she said firmly. "You be a good girl now. Whoa, there, whoa, there—"

Then they were at the bottom of the slope. Sarah could breathe again. Safe. Hyacinthe slowed a bit as they went rumbling over the wooden bridge. Then she threw herself forward again to climb the opposite hill, and soon they were up—up and over! There were the grain elevators of Blakely. They looked tall and proud, five giants guarding the town.

Hyacinthe was trotting across the tracks when a train locomotive wailed. It was at the crossing, half a mile away, but Hyacinthe was startled. She leaped, then galloped jerkily. Sarah clutched at the rod beside her to keep from being tossed out. Mother's knuckles were white again. She spoke sharply to the horse.

They swung onto the main street. And now it was fun to go whirling along. There were about six cars lined up in front of the stores!

I guess they can't go much faster than Hyacinthe, thought Sarah proudly.

Hyacinthe came to a stop in front of the station. A man came to lift the five-gallon can of cream and the two crates of eggs from the back of the buggy.

"Just in time for the 2:10 train," said the man.

Mother drove Hyacinthe across to the hitching posts. She had to hurry to tie up. The train was awfully close, and Hyacinthe's eyes were rolling again. She didn't like locomotives as much as Sarah did.

Oh, but it was splendid! The way the bell rang, the clouds of steam and smoke came hissing out, and the long whistle blew. Shivers raced up and down Sarah's back as the shiny black monster pounded past. Coach after coach came sliding out from behind the station now.

"Well, child!" called Mother laughing. She was halfway across the wide street, but Sarah still stood there, staring. "Coming?"

"Coming!" Sarah skipped to catch up. Watching the train was one happy thing about coming to Blakely. The second was almost as nice. It belonged to going to Jensen's store. If you stood just inside the door and closed your eyes, you could smell—oh, a lot of lovely smells. Moth balls—cheese—onions—apples—soap—leather—candy—

The candy reminded Sarah. She was rich today. She had five whole pennies to spend! Stuart had given them to her.

For five cents you could buy fifteen licorice jawbreakers— or two bars of chocolate with nuts inside—or twelve ounces of mixed hard candy. After long and serious thought Sarah chose the bag of candy. You could share it—and yet keep a lot. The candy lasted long too. Best of all, Mr. Jensen's Special had his name—J. J. Jensen—running clear through each candy stick, from end to end. It was like magic.

Sarah's dress pocket had a comfortable bulge when she and Mother walked down to the post office. Miss Hettie Burdock teased her about it, but not for long. Miss Hettie had news. She was eager to spill it. She leaned across to whisper importantly.

"How did you hear about it, Miss Hettie?" said Mother a bit stiffly.

"One of them postcards came. Anybody can read 'em." Miss Hettie wasn't embarrassed in the least. "Said there clear as could be. Miss Jane Bolton's niece is coming to live with her. I guess she would be about Sarah's age."

A thrill went tingling up Sarah's spine again. She'd have a friend to play with at last!

CHAPTER 2

A Skeleton—and a Mystery

Dᴉᴅ Mɪss Hᴇᴛᴛɪᴇ see the gladness in Sarah's eyes?

"Well, child," she said. " 'Tain't likely to do *you* much good if Miss Jane Bolton does have a girl livin' with her. An' pity the poor thing. That's what everybody says."

Mother had been buying stamps. She tucked them into her bag.

"Jane Bolton's my friend, Hettie," she said gently.

Sarah's mouth dropped open. She glanced at her mother. Then she shut her mouth again slowly.

"You were goin' to say somethin', lovey?" Miss Hettie's beady eyes looked eagerly at Sarah.

"I—Aunt Jane is awfully good to me."

"*Aunt Jane.* Well, now. You and your mother visits her real frequent, I s'pose?"

"We—I—"

"I'm afraid we have a good deal of business to do today, Miss Hettie—and here come some customers for you. We mustn't detain you. Good day, Hettie," said Mother with cheerful firmness.

The postmistress chuckled. "Some family skeletons ain't so all-fired secret, Sheila Scott," she called, still laughing. "You needn't think it!"

What did Miss Hettie mean? Sarah longed to ask it. But Mother seemed to have dismissed the postmistress from her mind. She had business at the blacksmith shop, she said, and at the Pool grain elevator, and the lumberyard—for Father. Sarah might go where she pleased for the next hour or so, just so she kept in sight of Hyacinthe and the buggy

Sucking a J. J Jensen Special, Sarah wandered solemnly toward the railway track. She should be excited about the girl coming to Aunt Jane's. And she was. But why did Mother never go to see Miss Jane Bolton? *She is my friend,* she told Miss Hettie. And Mother always told the truth. This seemed a bit like a lie though. Mother never—just *never*—went to see Aunt Jane. And Aunt Jane never came to the Scott home. She was kind to Sarah and Robbie though. She often stopped them on the way to or from school, just to talk a bit and feed them cookies and milk.

Sarah looked along the tracks, then she crossed them slowly.

A family skeleton. Was that a sad sort of secret? If it was, then the Scott family had one too. Six years ago, when Sarah was only four, her big brother Keith was angry with Father, dreadfully angry. He walked out of the house and all the way to Blakely. He got on the train—and he never came back.

Sarah wasn't sure she remembered her runaway brother at all. Robbie did. Robbie talked about him sometimes when they were alone. But not often. It made her feel too sad.

There was a picture of him in Mother's dresser drawer. Sometimes Sarah would sit on the floor beside the dresser, dreaming over the picture. Keith was handsome and tall, and when he laughed he showed his flashing white teeth.

Sometimes Sarah thought she could remember him like that.

No letters ever came from Keith. But every evening in his prayer, Father said, "And bless our absent loved one. Keep him safe—and draw him to Thee."

That was about the only time anyone ever mentioned him aloud in the Scott home anymore.

So maybe Keith was a skeleton. Was that what Miss Hettie meant? But hers seemed to have something to do with Aunt Jane Bolton.

Aunt Jane lived a mile from the Scotts. Less than a mile if you cut across the field. They were on the same party line too. But she and Mother never telephoned each other to ask about cake recipes, and what to do when your little chicks got sick, or what to do if the cream wouldn't turn to butter in the churn.

It was a sober prairie princess who climbed into the buggy when Mother was ready to start for home. Father had given her the nickname because Sarah meant "princess." Sometimes she daydreamed of what it would be like to be a real princess. She would wear white satin dresses trimmed with lace, every single day of the year! And every day she'd have homemade ice cream with angel food cake! But today she sat beside Mother, and she knew she really wished for just two things—no *Scott skeleton* and a really truly best friend of her own.

Hyacinthe was anxious to get out of harness, so she was especially hard to manage. It was worse when a car came chugging past. Their horns were so croaky, and their curtains flapped and fluttered, and a long trail of dust followed them. Hyacinthe sneered at cars. She thought it was her duty to race each one. Once she almost crowded into the

roadside ditch in her eagerness. Sarah clung to the dashboard of the buggy, thrilled and frightened.

But when they turned down the last halfmile lane, the spring silence settled around them. Hyacinthe trotted steadily. No one raced her. No one worried her. The reins flipflapped smartly, and the high buggy wheels gave out a pleasant whirring sound.

"Penny for your thoughts, Sarah," said Mother, breaking a long silence.

Sarah's heart gave a funny little flutter. Maybe this was the time to ask some question.

"Well, um—I was thinking. About what Miss Hettie said—and what you said. You said you were Aunt Jane's friend—"

"I am. I was—and I am. I always will be. What happened cannot change that."

"But what *happened*, Mother? Why isn't Aunt Jane *your* friend?"

"I'm—not sure." She spoke musingly. "I can guess."

"Tell!"

Mother shook her head. "I can't. For two reasons. I am not sure I know the real reasons—or the reasons within reasons. And if I did, it's Aunt Jane's affair, not mine."

"But—" Sarah looked unhappily at the silky pussy willows along the water-filled ditches they were passing.

"But what, dear?"

"But doesn't it hurt when you lose a friend?"

"It hurts. Deeply. Sarah, Aunt Jane and I were close friends from the time we were your age. My father was poor. Hers was well-to-do. That never made the slightest difference. We were inseparable. Some people thought her haughty. She—well, if she had one fault in my eyes it was that she sometimes found it hard to forgive people. Not me," added Mother quickly, "she was never anything but warm and generous toward me."

Mother's voice fell silent. For a while there was nothing but the clip-clop of hooves and the whir of wheels.

"And then?" said Sarah, unable to bear the suspense any longer.

"Well, when the break came I was hurt. At first. I had done her no wrong that I knew of. Then I went to her to try to make things right. It was no use. She refused to see me, or to speak to me. So I asked God to show me a way to show her that I loved her just the same."

"Did He?" said Sarah in an awed whisper.

Mother smiled thoughtfully. "I think He did." She was

silent for a bit. "Sometimes we face situations that we can't help—except by prayer. There's always prayer—for a Christian. It's a wonderful thing to be a Christian, Sarah. Whoa, there, Hyacinthe."

They were at home.

Kathleen emerged from the barn carrying two pailfuls of foamy milk. Robbie came running to take care of Hyacinthe. And Father took the bundles from Mother's arms, and walked toward the house with them. He had a nice smell of horses and hay and earth. The windmill squeaked, its blades whirling as it pumped water, filling the big tank. Stuart gave the two long whistles that were a call to the horses to come and drink. And now they came thundering from the far end of the pasture—twenty-three horses and yearling colts. Watching them was almost as good as watching the locomotive. Maybe even a bit better!

But it was almost suppertime, and Sarah had chores to do. She climbed to the hayloft to look for stray eggs. She fed the goslings and coaxed the woolly things into the wooden box that was their home for the night. Then she draped a horse blanket over the top to keep them warm. They had no mother goose to do it for them.

Saturday night was a family sort of time in the Scott home. The kitchen floor was shiny clean. The big room smelled clean. Eight big loaves of bread were cooling on the cabinet, crackling as they cooled. That was part of Saturday night sounds. Another was the snip-snap of scissors and the clickety-click of clippers as Father cut Stuart's and Robbie's hair, over in the corner that was farthest from the cabinet. Last of all Mother would trim Father's hair, and sweep up the clippings.

Kathleen was turning the handle of the new De Laval

cream separator—up and down, up and down, sixty times a minute. A thread of cream came spinning from the thin spout, and skim milk frothed from the other. The quiet hum had a rich important sound too. And then, when Sarah helped Robbie feed the calves, there was the slurping sound as they drank the skim milk, and butted the pails with baby horns.

But the best sound of all would come after supper—

Supper. Fluffy slices of new bread, spread with new butter! Mugfuls of cold, cold skim milk. Fried ham. Baked potatoes and gravy. Home-canned applesauce for dessert. Nobody hurried. The chores were all done. On Saturday nights Sarah usually had a cozy this-is-my-family feeling. Tonight she couldn't help wondering about the *skeleton*. Where was he right now and was he maybe thinking of home?

"Father?" She tugged at his sleeve to draw his attention.

"Yes Princess Sarah?"

"Did we have singing on Saturday night when—when *Keith* was at ho—" She gulped and swallowed the rest of the sentence. Father's face had grown terribly sad-looking. Stuart stared at his plate. Robbie was frowning and shaking his head at her. Sarah flushed and hung her head.

But Mother said quickly, "There's no reason why you should not mention Keith's name, dear. He is your brother. Yes, we had singing then too."

It had been going on for years and years!

Every Saturday evening the Scott family would cluster around the parlor organ. Sometimes neighbors dropped in. The Heathes, maybe. Or the Thatchers. Best of all, Sarah thought, were the times when the Scotts were alone. Stuart sang bass. Imagine! His voice was deep, and it hardly wobbled at all. Father sang tenor, and Mother was proud of his voice. Mother and Sarah and Robbie carried the melody. Kathleen took the alto, just the way she did in the choir. She could sing like anything!

Her fingers were sort of stubby. But her hands could hop smartly up and down the keyboard, and her pumping feet made the notes roll out good and strong, so they sent tickles racing up your back.

The organ was lovely. The tall back reached almost to the ceiling. It had a lot of fancy cutouts and carvings—leaves and things. There was a mirror in the middle, and a lamp bracket on each side. Sarah was proud to see the sparkling lamp globes even during the day. *She* had washed and shined them.

But in the evening! The light burned clear. It threw funny shadows on the flowered wallpaper. Robbie's cowlick looked about two times as long as it really was. And Kathleen's shadow was *big*—big as a storybook giant. It bobbed and swayed as she pumped and played and sang.

They would sing, "There's a new name written down in glory!" And, "Oh, come to the church in the wildwood—" Stuart would go, "Oh, come, come, come, come, come—" On and on, all the way through the chorus. It had a tramping sound. But the other voices went skipping along, sort of— "No spot is so dear to my childhood as the little brown church in the vale."

They sang about heaven, and about Jesus dying on the cross, and about marvelous grace— Not Grace Millar. *She* wasn't so marvelous, even if maybe she thought she was! This word *grace* was hard to explain. But Sarah *thought* she almost knew what it meant. They sang everybody's favorite, and then they went all around the circle again.

Just when Sarah wished they would never stop, the telephone gave one long ring. That meant that Central was closing for the day, and no more calls could be made

"Nine o'clock," said Father. "Tomorrow's Sunday, and we must be up early. Where's the Bible, Mother?"

After Bible-reading and prayer time, Father carried the big bathtub into the kitchen. Sarah got first turn. Then in her freshly washed nightgown she scampered up the stairs. There was a clean flour-sack sheet on the bed, and clean flour-sack pillowcases covered the pillows. They were still warm from being out in the sun most of the day, and they smelled of spring winds. Kathleen—or somebody—had patched the hole in Sarah's nightgown too.

For a thank-you, Sarah tucked a J. J. Jensen Special under Kathleen's pillow. Would she be surprised! Sarah giggled as she snuggled down.

The straw mattress rustled under her. Through the open window came the sound of birds cheeping and frogs croaking, and trees murmuring— In a minute Sarah was fast asleep.

CHAPTER 3

Safely Through Another Week

Sarah SQUINTED SLEEPILY at the shaft of sunlight that fell across her pillow.

"Hurry up, slowpoke," the sun seemed to be saying.

From the fence post almost directly below the open window came the meadowlark's call.

"When—are—you—all—gettin'—up?" it wanted to know.

Sarah giggled, and the giggle awoke Kathleen.

Kathleen yawned. "Why don't you let me sleep?"

Just that minute they heard the thud-thud of Father walking barefooted across the kitchen downstairs. Then came the rattle as he shook down the ashes in the cooking range. He was lighting the fire. Sarah heard the sputtering crackle of kindling burning, and smelled a whiff of smoke. Then he was pouring water into the water kettle and the porridge pot. Time to get up.

"Oh, well," sighed Kathleen as she rolled to a sitting position.

But Sarah bounded out of bed. Sunday morning was a hurry-hurry morning at the Scotts'. They lived five miles from church, and there were so many chores to do beforehand.

Sarah never could decide: Did the animals all know it was Sunday? The horses must know, in a way. This was the time all of them—except Prince and Captain—got to spend the whole long day in the meadow. They stood in bunches under the trees, swishing flies and getting each other to scratch their itchy places with their teeth. Or they raced, sweeping round and round the meadow like a band of overgrown colts. The rest of the time they cropped the grass.

Maybe that's what made the cows so cross. Kathleen said they always were hardest to milk on Sunday mornings. But Mother said that probably was because they could sense that she was in a hurry. It made them nervous.

Spencer knew. Somehow he knew. He couldn't know about church—about Father being Sunday school superintendent, and Brother Hammond preaching, and Kathleen singing in the choir. He probably wondered what they all did, away from home for hours and hours. Every Sunday morning he knew this was his lonesome day. Maybe Prince told him. Every Sunday morning, when Sarah hurried to feed the chicks and goslings, and when Robbie ran out with the skim milk to feed the calves, Spencer followed along, sniffing sadly. They patted his head, feeling sorry for him—and just a bit sorry for themselves too.

Because Sunday was a mixed kind of day—glad and sad. "Safely through another week," the Scotts always sang around the breakfast table. "Let us now His blessings seek, Waiting in His cords [courts] today. . . ." Sarah didn't know exactly what *cords* meant, but it sounded like being tied up. And that was the way Sunday felt, in a way.

Like wearing Sunday shoes. They were nice to look at—but *stiff!* And Sarah's feet practically melted, they were so hot. She sat in church, swinging them—but not too much. If she did, someone's hand came to rest on her knees, warning her to stop. The feet wanted and *wanted* to be running—over grass and over cool sand—and to go splashing through the creek. But they couldn't. This was Sunday.

"Quit your dreaming, Princess," said Father this morning. "Eat up your porridge. In an hour we must be on our way—"

"Hurry, dry the cups! What makes you so slow?" said Kathleen. "In half an hour we must go!"

"Let me fasten your hair ribbon," said Mother. "Do stand still for a minute, dear. Stuart is hitching the team to the buggy. Be careful how you put on your coat, and how you sit—so your sash won't be too badly crushed. There, now! Remember! Where's Kathleen?"

"Upstairs. Making earpuffs," said Sarah as she scooted for the door.

The buggy was waiting at the garden gate. Father and the boys were sitting there in their best suits and hats. Sarah stooped to pat Spencer's head.

"We'll be back again. In about four hours. Ah, come on! That's not so awfully long to wait, is it?" she whispered coaxingly.

He thought it was, and licked her fingers sadly.

Father helped Sarah and Mother over the high rear wheel. The three of them would sit in the back seat today because Stuart was driving. Prince was a slender bay, Captain a chunky sort of sorrel. They didn't match at all. But they were pretty good trotters. Now they had grown tired of waiting. They chewed their bits and tossed their manes, snorting. It's not a good thing to keep horses waiting.

"Kath*leen!*" called Mother.

She came—not running. Kathleen never ran anymore.

She was a young lady! Her earpuffs were just right. She never wore big oriole nests the way some girls did. She'd be ashamed to.

"You certainly took your time," grumbled Stuart.

"Less than you!" Kathleen flashed back. Her dark eyes could flash like anything too. The red cherries on her hat jiggled as she climbed to her seat. "After all, I had to wash the dishes and the separator, and—"

"That will do, Kathleen," said Mother quietly.

Stuart shook the reins and Prince and Captain were off.

The road had that bouncy feeling today, because this was spring and the earth still was cushiony with moisture. There wasn't much dust in the air—except when cars went scudding past. The Heathes passed. Not going to church. They never went to church. Their horn croaked and the curtains flapped. Maimie Heathe's scarf flapped and fluttered too.

"A sedan coming," shouted Robbie, swiveling his head. "A brand new car. Hey, who do you suppose—"

It came purring past. Through the dust cloud Sarah saw the grand car. Imagine! *Glass windows* on all sides! Why, you could ride along at maybe thirty-five miles an hour. Three times as fast as Prince and Captain were going. *Four* times! And you'd never get dusty at all!

"Lookit who's at the steering wheel!" yipped Robbie.

Aunt Jane Bolton! You'd never believe it. She was sitting erectly, looking straight ahead, though the car wobbled a bit. Aunt Jane—with a brand-new car. And a sedan! Of course, she was rich enough.

Sarah's heart turned over with envy. Now just about everybody had a car—everybody except the Scotts.

She sighed.

"Why so doleful, Princess? On such a lovely Lord's Day morning, too."

Princess. She felt more like a beggar girl.

"Listen to the meadowlark praising the Lord," said Mother dreamily. "If you rode in a closed car you'd never hear it."

And you wouldn't smell the pussy willows and crocuses, nor feel the gentle breeze tickling your neck, and the sunlight caressing your cheek. Most of all you couldn't pet a car and tickle its ears and feed it carrots. Sarah giggled at the thought, immensely comforted. Prince and Captain were her friends.

"We'll have a car too one of these days," promised Father.

"Well, but, *when?*"

"When we can afford it. Given a few good crops and fair prices, the day may come sooner than you'd think."

Captain's and Prince's ears went up suddenly. The church bell was ringing! They took the last half-mile slope smartly. The buggy whirled onto the grassy church yard and up to the hitching post. Father helped Mother and the girls down. The boys tethered the team and got out the oat sheaves. Father didn't linger. The superintendent had to be in his place on time.

Waiting for Sunday school to begin, Sarah's thoughts went over Father's promise again. She couldn't help wondering if the Thatchers could afford their car. Or the Gerricks. Maybe "afford" didn't always mean the same thing. Sadie Siddons said they couldn't afford to eat meat at their house. They had it only once in a while, because they sold all their pigs and chickens. But they bought candy—gobs and slathers of candy. They had chocolate bars just about every week.

Father couldn't *afford* candy more than about four times a year. But he bought Mother the new washer. Mrs. Siddons had to use the washboard all the time. Mother's washer had a large wheel on the side that you could turn, so the washing got done with hardly any rubbing at all! And Father built a cistern, and bought a pump—and the cream separator—and a windmill—

It was a good thing you didn't have to buy a voice. Father had a big tenor, and that was a great help in Sunday school. The church organ was old. It sounded, Mother once said, as if it had asthma. It gasped and coughed. The minister's wife, Sister Hammond, played. Once or twice she screwed up her face, as if the organ gave her a toothache. But Father's voice led out good and strong, so the singing wasn't too bad.

"There is sunshine in my soul today—"

Sister Hammond was Sarah's teacher this year. Last year she'd had Mrs. Eggermaier. *She* asked many questions—and you were supposed to read the answers out of your Bibles. Like this· "What did Jesus say to His disciples? What did they answer? What did He say to the Pharisees? What did they ask Him? What did He answer? What did His disciples ask Him next?" It was baby stuff. Sister Hammond had sparkly eyes in a pincushion face. She made you think, *hard*. She looked as if she thought the Bible was the most exciting book in the world. And it was. But—

Well, parts of it could make you uncomfortable. Today's lesson was about the one lost sheep Sister Hammond had tears in her eyes as she told of how the Shepherd went out to find the sheep. He wouldn't give up, and He *couldn't* give up, until He'd found it.

She's talking about you, Sarah Naomi, said a voice deep inside her.

She's not! I'm not lost!

You are, Sarah Naomi. You are!

You be quiet! thought Sarah crossly.

Then she felt a tiny bit frightened. *What if I was talking to—to the Shepherd? What if He should stop—* But she wasn't going to think about it anymore.

During Sunday school the church was divided into little squares, one square to each window. Each "room" had curtain walls of brown brocade. The voices of all the teachers and their pupils bounced over and under and

through the curtains. So it was easy to let your mind slip away from what your teacher was saying.

Sarah stared intently at the brocade. It looked like palm trees or ferns. A tropical forest! Suddenly she was walking through the forest—and she came to a castle. A lovely princess lived there. She had long golden curls, and sky-blue eyes, and lovely pearly teeth, and hundreds of servants, and—

"Sarah?"

She started. The castle collapsed. The forest dwindled. They turned back into a swaying brocade curtain again. Sister Hammond was looking expectantly at her.

Sarah flushed. "Uh—I—I'm s-sorry. I didn't hear—"

"Have you memorized a Bible verse for today?"

She shook her head. "I'm—I'm sorry—"

It wasn't true. Only yesterday she learned, "All we. like sheep have gone astray—" But suddenly she couldn't say it. The verse was *wrong*. It couldn't be right. *She* wasn't lost!

Sarah was glad when Sunday school was over today. Brother Hammond had a good sermon—all about Jehoshaphat who marched singing into battle, and how God fought for him. It was exciting.

At the door later he held Sarah's hand for a moment. "It does my heart good to see how attentive you are to God's Word, my dear," he said. And he shook the hand, smiling.

Sarah smiled back, but she felt a bit panicky. She was glad Sister Hammond was collecting hymnbooks at the organ. *She* knew better! *She* knew Sarah wasn't attentive all the time. But she hadn't heard. Quickly as possible

Sarah slipped over to where her mother was talking to Mrs. Gerrick.

She was inviting the Gerrick family over for dinner. Susan stood by too. The girls hugged one another when Mrs. Gerrick said she would speak to her husband about it.

She did. He said yes—but they'd have to go home first to feed the chicks and see if the baby pigs were all right. Sarah got to ride home in the Gerrick car, too.

It gave you a funny tickly feeling, swooshing along at thirty-five miles an hour! Sometimes going down a little hill they even went forty! And they took the long round-about way so as not to get to the Scott place ahead of the buggy. This was an exciting drive.

When Sarah arrived at home she hopped down. Politely she invited the Gerricks into the house. Mother came to the door to greet her guests.

In the kitchen Kathleen was flying around, setting the table, making coffee, slicing the cold roast, frying potatoes, creaming peas, cutting company cake—

Serving cake was a real elegant thing—almost as elegant as having a car!

CHAPTER 4

Sunday Company

SARAH WAS ANXIOUSLY counting plates on the table. Four at each side—two at each end—twelve! There were six Scotts. And Mr. and Mrs. Gerrick, and Ralph, and Chuck, and Bertie, and Susan—twelve! Goody!

"Herbie's coming too," announced Susan. She was speaking to Kathleen's back.

"Oh?" Kathleen went on stirring the potatoes.

Susan ought to know better than to talk to a person who is busy! Besides, Sarah couldn't see why Herbie should bother to come. It wasn't as if he *had* to go places with the family. He had his own car—a little runabout with a rumble seat! And it wasn't as if there was anyone here for him to visit. He was real old. About twenty-three!

"There's the runabout now," squeaked Susan, running to the window. "No. It isn't. It's—"

Before she could say the name Stuart poked his head into the kitchen from the entry.

"Father!" he called. "Father! The Thatchers are here."

Sarah looked at Robbie. He looked back at her. Both of them groaned softly.

"Second table," said Robbie resignedly.

At the start he had taken Susan's three brothers upstairs

36

to the boys' room. But every minute dinner smells grew stronger. So every minute the four boys had come edging farther and farther down the stairs. They were sitting on the third and fifth steps from the bottom now, peering through the railing at the table that was filling up with eats. But Robbie rose to lead the way back up now. If you ate at the second table you had to wait *an hour,* at least.

But then, after all, they didn't have to wait. The Thatchers hadn't brought anyone except Louise. She was redheaded, and sort of tomboyish. She sang alto in the choir, and she went to high school in town. She and Stuart were both in grade 11. But she was good friends with Kathleen, who had never been to high school at all.

Louise would really *rather* wait with Kathleen, she said. And Stuart said he wasn't very hungry, which was sort of surprising. And Herbie Gerrick just smiled and said he could afford to wait— So there was room at the table for everyone else.

After dinner Sarah didn't even need to help with dishes. Mother told her to run along and play.

Spencer was happy about that. He raced and tumbled round and round them all the way down the hill to the creek and the strawstack.

The Scotts always had the most monstrous strawstack in the whole countryside. That was because Father hated hauling straw in winter to bed and feed the cattle. Instead of threshing here and there out on the field, the way other farmers did, he threshed all the grain at the foot of the hill near the creek. This meant he had to hire extra men, because the sheaves had to be brought from such distances. But that was all right.

The big machine coughed up all the straw and piled it

in a mountainous heap. When the cold weather set in in fall, the cattle simply ate their way into the pile. They ate out rooms and passages where they could be snug even if a three-day blizzard was blowing.

But this was spring. You could hardly believe there ever had been any snow. The cattle were lying down today, in the shade of the whispering trees. The strawpile passages were nice scary shadowy places for a game of hide-and-seek. Susan's brothers and Robbie played there with the girls for a while. Then they went wandering off down the creek, taking Spencer with them.

Sarah and Susan decided to climb the stack.

A strawstack in spring is just about the most slippery climb in the world. The sun and the winds and the weight of the snow have made the walls and dome slick as anything. Today there was a brisk wind blowing too. That was no help.

They worked their fingers into the stack and grabbed a hold. Inch by inch they would fight their way. Without warning their shoes would *slip*—and there they hung. Not for long. Laughing, they dropped to the bottom again. There was a thick layer of straw all around, so they couldn't really get hurt.

And they didn't give up. They started over about ten times, going a bit higher at each try. And just at the last, the wind blew over the top of the pile, into their faces, pushing with all its might. They threw themselves forward. And they were at the top. They really were.

And there was a little hollow! You couldn't see it from below.

"How about that!" said Sarah. "I think Robbie made the hollow. He said he and Spencer had a hideout, and he

wouldn't tell me where it was. I've found it. I just know
I have."

It was warm and cozy here. If you didn't raise your head
the wind just scooted over you, hardly touching you at all.
But you could see far. You could look right onto Aunt
Jane Bolton's yard. The bedding was still sunning on the
line.

This reminded Sarah, and she began to tell about the
girl that was coming to live at Aunt Jane's. But Susan
knew. She had heard. Miss Hettie must have told just
about *everybody*. But Susan wasn't excited and happy
about the news the way Sarah was.

"Why not?" said Sarah.

"Because you're going to be best friends with her. I
just know you are. You'll live so close. And I want you
and *me* to be best friends. Because—because— Come close
and I'll whisper."

"Why? Nobody's going to hear. I don't like whispering.
It tickles."

"Well, then, I won't tell!"

"I don't care!" Susan was becoming so bossy! She always
wanted to do things her way, and no way else.

"That's a fib," said Susan. "You *do* care!"

"I don't!"

"You do!"

"I don't!"

"You do—you do—you do—you do—you do—you do—
you do—you do—"

"I don't—I don't—I don't—I don't—I don't—"

They chanted it faster and faster till they were out of
breath. Then they giggled and were friends again. Sarah
even let Susan whisper in her ear.

"Herbie's sweet on Kathy. That's why he's here today."

Sarah's mouth dropped open in surprise and dismay. Herbie Gerrick. He was—he was nobody *special*. Just Herbie Gerrick. He had a chubby moon face like his dad. A bit like Susan's. He never said much, or so it seemed to Sarah. He had a farm, and a runabout, and that was all. He worked with his father.

But Kathleen— Why, she was going to marry an *important* man some day. That's what *she* always said.

"Well, she's not sweet on him!" declared Sarah.

"She is so!"

"Who said?"

"Herbie. I heard him talking to Ma and Pa!"

"Herbie!" Sarah sniffed scornfully. "He doesn't know."

"He does so!"

"He doesn't. He *can't!*"

"He does—he does—he does—"

They were chanting again until they were breathless, but this time there was no giggling finish. They just sank into silence because they were tired.

"And I'll tell you something else. I know why Miss Bolton's mad at your mother, all these years. Want me to tell?"

Sarah shouldn't listen. This was gossip. Mother said the secret was Aunt Jane's, and she said you must never listen to gossip. But— Sarah *was* curious to know.

"Your father was Miss Bolton's father's hired man. My mother said. And she wanted to marry him—and—"

"Your *mother?*"

"No! Silly. Miss Bolton. And he wouldn't. He married her best friend—that's your ma. And that's why she's mad, and why she never comes to church anymore. And that's why you can't be best friends with that girl who's going to live with her. You'd better be best friends with me. If Herbie and Kathy get married—"

"Her name is *Kathleen*," said Sarah loftily. "And they won't. They never will."

"They will so. You'll see. Then you and me just about *gotta* be best friends. We'll be one family, sort of."

Sarah jumped to her feet. Whew! How the wind did blow!

"Let's roll down the stack," she suggested daringly. She thought Susan would never do it.

"Let's," said Susan.

Sometimes it may be a good thing to be a sort of butterball—like Susan. She rolled down smoothly as anything. Sarah bounced from elbow to elbow. The sky and the trees, the creek and the grass, the cows and the horses— everything went spinning jerkily around, like mad. Then— bump! Sarah lay still, her eyes closed.

A moment later she heard a whine, and a warm wet something flicked all over her face. Her eyes flew open. She sat up laughing, her arms going around Spencer's neck. He had come back to her!

"Did you think I was hurt? Well, I'm not. Come on, Susan, let's run up to the house."

They brushed straw from their hair and dresses as they scampered up the hill.

At the garden gate they stopped short. Sarah's mouth dropped open in dismay. Susan was grinning. There were just four people on the porch. Herbie and Stuart, Kathleen and Louise. Herbie sat on the step at Kathleen's feet, leaning against the post and strumming a banjo. And Louise was sitting in the swing, playing a guitar. All of them were singing, " 'Tis the last rose of summer—"

Silly! When this was springtime! And the way Herbie sang the tenor sounded like, " 'Tis the la-hast ro-ho-hose of suh-hummer—" *Susan* thought it sounded wonderful. You could see it on her face. She smiled as she went up the walk.

Sarah marched soberly past the four music-makers and into the kitchen. New trouble greeted them there.

"Eeeek!" shrieked Mrs. Gerrick faintly when she saw the girls.

"Sarah Naomi Scott!" gasped Mother. "Where *have* you been?"

Both mothers made grabbing motions, pulling straw bits out of hair and stockings and shoes.

"Your shoes are simply ruined!" wailed Mother.

They were pretty badly scraped. "I'm s-sorry," muttered Sarah.

"Well, this settles it," said Mrs. Gerrick decidedly. "Susan has to change completely before the evening meeting. We'll not be staying on for supper."

Mother felt bad about that, but Sarah watched her friend go with a feeling of relief. She longed for her secret hiding place under the big crab apple tree. It was lovely just now, all pink and perfumy with blossoms. And it was quiet. And private. But how to get there? She wasn't going to tramp past the music-makers again.

Sarah tiptoed into her parents' bedroom and opened the window. It stuck for a while, but she managed to push it just far enough so she could wriggle through and drop to the ground.

She ran softly across the grass and along the orchard walk.

She was just about to dive into her hidey-hole when she ran smack into—*Father!*

"Whoa, my young filly!" His arms caught and held her. "Well, Princess Sarah Naomi. Am I mistaken—or do you have problems on your mind?" His hard brown hands cupped her face for a moment. "Is it anything you care to tell your father?"

"Let me go," she whispered, trying to twist free. *"Let me go!"*

His arms dropped. She was free. But when she saw his face she couldn't slip away. He looked so concerned, and sorry.

"Is it very bad?"

She nodded, nibbling the inside of her cheek.

"It's awful! *I* don't believe it's true—but Susan says it is. And *I* think you should tell that Herbie Gerrick to take that old runabout off the yard and never, never come back!"

Father's lips twitched. Then he was shaking with silent laughter, shaking and holding her, with tears slipping down his cheeks.

"So that's the way the wind blows," he said, wiping his eyes, and chuckling aloud now.

He was going to side with Herbie! Sarah was so mad she told him the other part—about Miss Bolton and Mother and all.

"Whoa, there," said Father soberly now. "You've evidently been listening to gossip. But about your sister—Princess, it hurts to think of her leaving the home nest. That's only natural. But her going is natural too. God planned it that way."

"T-to *H-Herbie's?*" quavered Sarah.

Father smiled—then he sighed a bit. "I hope they're not making a mistake. I trust they are seeking God's will. That is all that matters. Just to do His will. But come now—Cheer up, little sister. Kathleen will be making her home only two miles away. You can still see each other several times a week. And anyway, haven't I heard you mention that Kathleen is too bossy?"

"*Don't,* Father!"

He was sober instantly. His big hand smoothed her hair. "Poor little lost lamb!" he said. "Why, what's the matter *now?* Hey! Come back!"

But Sarah was darting away. "H-have to g-get ready f-for ch-church," she called over her shoulder.

He knows. Her heart was doing a pittery-pattery hop and skip *Father knows.* This was the most terrible part of the whole Sunday. She was *lost* and now she was sure that Father knew.

CHAPTER 5

Linda

Spring was the time for new things.
New black colts, speckled with silver, that trotted along on
rubbery legs—legs so long and thin they looked like stilts!
New clucking hens coming proudly off their nests, leading
about fifteen furry babies each.

Spring was a hurry-hurry time too. Father explained the
reason for that. In about ninety days the first autumn frost
would be nipping the grainfields. And the seed hadn't even
been sown yet!

That was why Stuart had to miss two weeks of school to
man the seeder while Father rode the plow. That was why
even Robbie had to do field work. Half school days now
and then, and all day Saturday. He walked after the harrow, over the plowed fields, back and forth, back and forth.
That was why Kathleen and Mother did such jobs as cleaning the barn, forking down feed and slopping the pigs.
And it was why Sarah had to teach the newest baby calves
how to drink their milk from a pail.

She had seen it done before. You stuck your right hand
into the milk with the fingers curving upward just a bit.
And you steered the stubborn little head down into the
pail with your left hand. Calves really tugged at your fingers when they sucked. And that was all right, if the calf

46

was a sensible baby. After a while it caught on and would slurp the warm milk without help from any fingers.

But Brindle's bony baby was as stubborn as his ma. He snorted and sneezed, and bunted around with his baby horns, until the pail spun out of her hand—and all the milk cascaded down her apron and dress.

"Stupid! Stupid! Stupid!" she wailed, stamping her drenched foot.

"Too bad, kiddie," came Kathleen's voice. "Gently, there! He doesn't know any better. I'll feed the rascal."

"But my dress! I'm soaked!"

Getting out of milky clothes is the *stickiest* thing. Anybody should know that!

"You'll have to go swimming in the creek with your goslings. Why don't you?" suggested Kathleen.

Sarah cheered up instantly. Taking the little geese down the hill was one daily chore that was real fun. All Sarah had to do was open the gate of their pen and call, "Peelee, peelee, peelee—"

Then she would walk ahead—and they would string out behind her. One foot up, one foot down, each webbed footstep placed exactly in front of the last. On they came waddling, waddling. If Spencer wasn't keeping Robbie company on the field, he would trot to the end of the rocking row, making sure no goslings got lost in the grass. If one got muddled, he nosed it gently back onto the path.

Today Sarah couldn't wait to get to the creek. Stockings and all she waded right into the stream and plunked down on a rock, up to her waist in the water. Let the rippling creek wash the milk away—

The goslings must have been surprised. They formed a gossipy circle around her, tipping their heads from side

to side as one eye and then the other took in the curious scene. *A girl in the creek.* Imagine! They nibbled at her billowy skirt, and at her toes. Sarah laughed.

"Go 'way! Shoo!"

When the water was running clear once more Sarah wrung out the skirt and apron as well as she could with her inside them. Then she trotted back and forth on the bank, and climbed some trees, swaying and rocking until the things were only dampish. It was time to go by then. Rounding up the goslings wasn't quite as simple as bringing them downhill. They always followed the current for a bit in their swim, and they didn't like going upstream again.

But the call "Peelee—peelee—peelee" meant things besides swim time. It meant supper. It meant a warm bed for night. Pretty soon one gosling would get the idea—and all the others followed. Out of the water. A quick shake of their stubby tails to scatter the wet drops. Then up the hill, into the pen, up to the feeding trough they waddled. There they gobbled food and made contented noises. Sarah could close the pen.

She was just in time, for her father and the boys were coming up the lane.

Three six-horse teams sure fill up a yard. Sarah darted in and out helping to unfasten buckles and to drag the harness parts aside for Father and the boys to hang up. She just knew the horses were aching for two things: a delicious roll on the grass to rest their tired shoulders and backs, and a long cool drink at the trough. When about a dozen draft horses are waving their hooves in the air at the same time, though, you'd better keep out of the way.

Supper was pretty late these days. And this Saturday evening, after Robbie had been walking behind the harrow all day, he fell asleep right in the middle of taking a bite of buttered bread.

"Poor laddie," said Father softly, and sighed. "So young to be shouldering such responsibility."

But Mother said, "He'll be bragging about this to his grandchildren one day."

Robbie a grandfather! thought Sarah.

Father left his supper for a bit. He steered Robbie to the woodshed where he got the tub of hot water ready. And he helped him with his bath. Then he steered him upstairs and into bed.

"I doubt if he really awoke at all," said Father, coming back to his unfinished supper.

That evening they sang softly, so as not to awaken Robbie. And after only about two songs Stuart said he'd better get some shut-eye.

Perhaps Stuart worked hardest of all. Louise Thatcher and the principal of Blakely high school were helping him to keep up with his classes. Every other evening or so Louise rode over to bring Stuart some notes. They were written on little cards, small enough so he could tuck them into the vest pocket of his dusty coveralls. History facts and dates—mathematic problems—things like that. And in the evenings, long after everyone else was asleep, Stuart would be studying in his room. Sarah knew. On Saturdays his lamp was the driest—*bone* dry—and his lamp chimney the smokiest of all. His eyes were red from the dust all day and the reading for hours at night.

So everyone was glad when Sunday came around. Everyone except Sarah. She wondered why. Why did she dread them? She used to like Sundays. But this spring every sermon and every Sunday school lesson made her uncomfortable. They were like jeering fingers pointing at her. Or like voices whispering, *This means you, Sarah Naomi.*

* * *

The weather really turned warm.

"Mayn't we go barefoot?" pleaded Robbie one morning.

"Not yet. It's too chilly this morning."

"But the Darnleys and the Slocum boys can. Why can't I?"

"No arguments, please. And be off with you now. It's past eight o'clock!"

Because Daisy and Beauty had new colts, Wally the old school horse was needed on the fields this spring. This meant that Robbie and Sarah had to walk to school. On a warm day, with shoes on, three miles is a long, long way to walk.

In school all the windows and the outer door were open wide today. This made a bit of cross draft, but not much. The water in the stone jar turned lukewarm. The pupils let the teacher prod and push them through arithmetic and spelling, reading and history— And then, *at last,* they heard,

"Put away your books. Stand!"

Gustily they obeyed. "Now the day is over—" they sang. School was dismissed.

It was so sultry, Robbie and Sarah didn't feel like talking on the way home. Their feet were steaming hot. Their tongues felt thick and sticky. Their shadows shuffled along ahead of them.

And then!

"Yippee!" yelled Robbie, pointing at a clump of yellow flowers in the ditch. Baptisia, the wild yellow sweet pea. The minute you saw the Baptisia in bloom you could shed your footwear. You needn't wait for permission. This was a Scott family rule!

Chuckling, the brother and sister flung themselves into the roadside grass and hurriedly unlaced their shoes. Off came the heavy ribbed stockings. Delightedly they wriggled their white toes.

Robbie knotted his shoelaces, and slung his shoes over his shoulder.

"Pooh! How can you stand the smell?" said Sarah.

"Huh! Girls are so fussy. At least I don't have to wave mine around like you."

They padded along the road, enjoying the feel of dust between their toes.

That was the day they found Miss Jane Bolton waiting for them in the shade of a poplar grove just a half mile from school. In her sedan! They got a ride almost all the way home! The shiny leatherette seat was a bit hot, but the rubber mat was cool under their bare feet, and with all the windows down, a breeze fanned them.

"I have a surprise for you," said Miss Bolton almost the moment they were seated. "My young niece is coming to live with me."

"Yes, we know," said Robbie.

Miss Bolton laughed shortly. "You do, do you? Just what do you know, I wonder?"

"Well, we heard things. Different things."

Different was right. The whole of Braeburn school buzzed with the story these days. The girl was twelve years old— She was not! She was seventeen!

She was starting school at Braeburn any day now— She wasn't coming at all, because she was too stuck-up to go to any country school— She couldn't speak English because she was born in India—or maybe it was Bolivia—

"I can imagine," said Miss Bolton dryly. Then she told them the *facts*.

The girl's name was Linda Bolton. She was eleven. She was born in Borneo—which sounded like a joke but wasn't. Her mother was dead. Her father was in the diplomatic service so he couldn't come home with her. But Linda— poor child—had had infantile paralysis—

"You mean—she's lame?"

Aunt Jane nodded as she threw Sarah a searching look. "Oh, poor Linda! We'd like to be her friends."

"Your parents won't—object?"

"Of course not! They'd want us to be!"

Aunt Jane's face wore a strange look for a moment. But all she said was, "I'm glad."

Linda was expected to arrive on the twenty-fifth of May.

"And," said Miss Bolton dryly, "you may tell your schoolmates that they've all been better informed than I—though I was the one who was doing the corresponding with my brother. Not until this very day did I know definitely that Linda was coming—and when. Well, good-bye."

May twenty-fifth. It was like a magic thing, a happy song. Linda was coming. She would be Sarah's very special friend. And maybe Aunt Jane and Mother would become *real* friends once more too.

Almost every day on the way home from school Sarah stopped at Aunt Jane's house now. The big downstairs bedroom was going to be Linda's. Aunt Jane papered it. There were pink and white and silver stripes with bunches of roses climbing all over. The curtains were white and misty-looking. The window frames and the furniture, all were painted white. There was a rose flounce around the dressing table, and a matching flounce around the bed. And on the bed was a pink and white flower quilt.

"It's—it's *beautiful*. Almost as nice as Linda's name. She's just going to love it—and *love* it!"

"You think so?"

"Of course! Why, she's just *got* to!"

The twenty-fifth was on Monday. Aunt Jane had asked Sarah to ask her mother if she might stop in for tea after school that day. Mother said she might.

She didn't mention the thing to Susan Gerrick though. Susan always got jealous the moment Sarah said a word about Linda. The secret was like a bubbly spring inside her.

On Sunday afternoon Herbie Gerrick came to lean against the Scott pillar at Kathleen's feet, and to strum his banjo and sing. Sarah didn't care—much. *Tomorrow,* she thought. *Tomorrow! Let* Kathleen get all moony about Herbie Gerrick. *She'd* have *Linda!*

But on Monday morning Father asked Mother to come to Paxton with him. That was the big town about twenty miles away.

"I can't. Kathleen will have her hands full with the laundry. She can't do the chores alone."

"Surely the Princess can help her," said Father, tweaking Sarah's nearest braid.

"Oh, no! Not me!"

"And why not?"

"This is the twenty-fifth! I've got to go to Aunt Jane's *directly* after school!"

They talked back and forth—but there was no help for it. Father had to go today and no other time. He needed Mother to make some important decisions. Sarah would just have to come home first before going to Aunt Jane's for tea.

This was going to spoil everything.

She had meant to be at Aunt Jane's when Linda arrived. She had known *exactly* how it was going to be. Linda would see Sarah waiting on the porch for her—and her pale and lovely face would break into a sad and lovely smile. And from that very minute they would be best friends. They would tell each other secrets, and it would be lovely. Now everything was going to be spoiled.

Wally, the school horse, was needed on the field—and so was Robbie. So Sarah would walk home from school. Three miles! And she would do chores after that—and walk another mile back to Aunt Jane's! It was too bad!

CHAPTER 6

The Magic Twenty-fifth

MAY TWENTY-FIFTH was another warm day. But this time Sarah didn't dawdle on the way home. She hurried so fast her face felt hot as an oven. Her hair was damp so it clung to her forehead. Coming up the drive she was panting like a little locomotive.

Kathleen was hanging out laundry. Sarah trotted past without a word. Up the walk—across the porch— The screen door slammed behind her. But no coolness awaited her in the house. Soap—and steam—and the smell of wet things— The kitchen was full of smells. The washer and the rinsing tubs took up most of the space. Sarah wriggled past to get to the water pail first of all. She raised a dipperful, cold and dripping, to her lips. Ah!

There was a heap of newly dried laundry—sheets and shirts and things—on the table. A big piece of cardboard was propped against the pile. *SARAH NAOMI* was scrawled across the top. Underneath it was a list of things to do. *Seven.* Sarah groaned aloud. Then she read:

1. Release the handle of the windmill. Fill the trough, but see to it that it does not overflow.

2. Toss twenty-five oat sheaves into the hay mow. Better use your hands. Fork tines are dangerous things.

3. Round up the cows. Fasten them in their stanchions.

4. Feed and water the goslings—as usual. They can skip their swim today though, don't you think?

5. Feed and water the mother hens and their broods. You know where the feed is, don't you? In a sack in the lean-to.

6. Fill the woodbox. Father split wood this morning.

7. Wash, tidy up—and slip into clean things. Surprise! It's lying on our bed. Then be off—and have a good time.

Sarah scampered upstairs. Whee! Her new school dress! Kathleen must have finished it this morning. Her blue print with the swirly skirt! Sarah spun around on her toes three times before diving down the stairs to begin her chores.

"Thank you!" she called to Kathleen as she trotted toward the barn.

Release handle of windmill. That was easy enough. If there was a stiff wind, shutting off the windmill was the tricky thing. Instantly now, high overhead, the metal plates groaned as they unfolded and swung to face the wind. Now they were spinning—fast and faster—and the first gush of cold water poured into the trough.

Sarah climbed to the loft.

Twenty-five oat sheaves. That was another quickie. You dragged the sheaves across the slippery hayloft floor, and you gave them a shove. Down they tumbled. Last of all you could drop onto the bouncy pile, not even bothering to use the ladder.

Round up the cows. That was Number 3. But sometimes the cows were dreadful slowpokes, and Spencer wasn't here to hint gently that he *might* nip their heels if they didn't get a wiggle on. He must be on the field with Robbie. And while she was gone the trough might overflow. So Sarah did the feeding and watering jobs next.

Things began to go wrong. Sarah was in too much of a *hurry*. She upset pans of water and had to run to refill them. She spilled feed, wasting some. And at the last, she upset a chicken coop. The startled mother hen fluttered away, screeching to her baby chicks to come away from the dangerous human. Sarah wished for Spencer. She had to do the circling now, running ahead, spreading her arms, shooing them gently back toward the coop. She got them penned just in time. The trough was almost overflowing. The wind played tricks too. The handle hauled Sarah right off her feet before it would snap down, shutting off the pump.

Everything was taking much too long. Something inside her kept urging. *Hurry, hurry, hurry!* By now, though, Sarah was much too tired to go trotting to the far end of the pasture for the cows. She plodded and plodded—fanning herself with her straw hat. The cows lay in the shade of the poplar grove, chewing their cud, and she just *knew* they wouldn't want to move now—

That moment she felt a cold nose poke into her hand. Spencer! He had seen her from the field and had come home to help her. Good old Spencer. Now everything was all right.

The cows never tried any nonsense when he was there. All he had to do was to give a faint *woof,* or maybe wave his tail. They lumbered to their feet now, groaning a bit. Brindle, the boss cow, swung to head for home. The others fell in line behind her.

One thing though— Spencer let them drink at the trough. This was the way he'd been taught to do. This was the way he did it. He wouldn't hurry them a bit. Sarah hopped impatiently from one foot to the other and back again. The cows took long lazy slurps of water. Finally Spencer got them headed for the barn and their own stanchions. Then, his chores done, he licked Sarah's hand, and trotted away to join Robbie once more.

Sarah's hands shook as she fastened the last pole in place. It was late, late, late, Past six o'clock!

A daring idea came to her while she was changing into her new dress and things. The more she thought of it the better she liked it. Hyacinthe was in the pasture. She was almost never used on the fields. She *was* a bit snuffy, but Sarah had ridden her bareback once or twice. And it wasn't really difficult to get the halter on her. Kathleen was in the barn, milking. She wouldn't notice.

Hyacinthe didn't like the idea quite as well as Sarah had. Twice on the way to Aunt Jane's she tried to turn back. At the last she was doing a fancy sort of sideways hop, with Sarah lying on her neck, grimly holding her head turned in the right direction.

"Mercy!" exclaimed Aunt Jane from the porch.

Sarah slid off, glad to feel the ground under her feet again. She tethered Hyacinthe to the gate post.

"I'm sorry I'm so late, Aunt Jane. But I *had* to go home to do chores. Did Linda come?"

"Yes." Aunt Jane sounded funny. Her glance slid down the front of Sarah's new dress. It was a bit rumpled. "Would you care to wash up a bit?"

"Guess so." It seemed a waste of time, though. She *had* washed. Just before she left home!

In the little washroom off the kitchen, Sarah splashed and

soaped quickly and buried her face in a thick towel that smelled of flowers.

"Care to comb your hair?" said Aunt Jane in the same funny voice.

Sarah turned to glance in the mirror. Her hair was a bit—well, messy. But you couldn't really comb it without opening the braids. Sarah didn't know how to redo them— and Aunt Jane didn't offer to. But to please her hostess Sarah ran the comb through the top quickly. There!

On the dining room sideboard she saw a trayload of pretty china and of sandwiches and things. The sight cheered her. This was going to be a real elegant tea. But most of all she wanted to bound into Linda's room with a cheery hello. Aunt Jane was tiptoeing, for some strange reason. Sarah found herself tiptoeing too.

Linda. There she was. Sitting in the armchair near the window. She was—oh, *lovely*. She had the blond hair and the sky-blue eyes— *Just* like a best friend in a storybook. But there was one difference. Linda's eyes didn't return Sarah's smile.

"Hello, Linda!" Sarah burst out breathlessly. "I'm Sarah Naomi Scott. And I've been waiting and waiting for you to come!"

"Oh? Hello." Just that, and no more. The cool greeting cut Sarah's words short.

And Aunt Jane wasn't much help. "I'll serve the lunch now—that is, the tea," she said, and she hurried away.

"It's late, you know," remarked Linda Bolton.

"I know. And I'm real sorry," said Sarah, feeling more uncomfortable by the minute. It was the kind of feeling she had when Miss Halliday reprimanded her in school—

for carelessness in writing, perhaps. But Linda was no teacher! She wasn't much older than Sarah, and not as big!

"I—I'm s-sorry," she said again.

"Well, being s-sorry doesn't really mend matters, you know. It's still late," said Linda.

Maybe she hadn't intended to imitate Sarah's stammer. Sarah couldn't tell. But suddenly a hot little candle-flame of anger leaped up inside her.

"I hurried. I had work to do. Lots of chores. I rode over fast as I could—"

Linda laughed a tinkly laugh. "If you can call it riding. In Borneo we used to go riding every morning, my dad and I. In real riding clothes and lovely saddles and everything— Oh, *why* did you have to go and remind me? I think it's hateful of you!"

Hasty words crowded to Sarah's lips. Then her glance fell on Linda's thin dangling legs and she bit back the words. Still it was a good thing that Aunt Jane brought in the tray just then. Sandwiches, tarts, cream puffs, cakes— It gave them something to do so words didn't matter. Sarah tried to remember not to be greedy. She was hungry!

Linda nibbled. She said she didn't feel like eating today. Her voice sounded weak and complaining.

Sarah began to wonder desperately what to talk about. She knew almost nothing about Borneo! And it wasn't safe to discuss horses. Her eyes swept slowly around the pretty room. Suddenly she caught sight of a row of dolls that sat on a shelf. Dolls in satin saris. Dolls in the prettiest Japanese kimonos. Dolls that looked like grown-up ladies, in stylish hats and dresses and real leather shoes.

"Oh!" She almost dropped her cup of tea. Hastily she

set it down. "Oooooh!" She bounded across the room for a closer look at the beauties.

"Don't touch them!" Linda shouted hoarsely. "You'll dirty them."

There was a shocked silence.

"Sarah, dear," Aunt Jane spoke up quickly. "Would you mind adding some hot water to the teapot? The water's boiling on the stove."

Sarah carried the teapot to the kitchen, glad to get away. She was jolted and puzzled and hurt. Not a single thing was going the way she had imagined it would. Not one single thing. Maybe Linda was tired from the trip. But she didn't really sound or look tired. She sounded just plain cross. Maybe she was lonesome, Sarah reminded herself. It must be dreadful to be separated from her father, and not to have any mother at all. Sarah knew what *her* mother would say if she were here:

"You'll need to be patient, dear."

"I'll tell her about my rag doll, Samanatha," she decided with an inward giggle as she approached Linda's room cautiously with the filled teapot. In the middle of the dining room she stood rooted. Linda's voice came to her clearly.

"Send her away! I don't want to see her. Not today, nor *ever!* She's— she's *awful*. She's *crude*. She smells. Horsey. And—and she came on that horrid beast because she knows I'll never be able to ride again."

"Hush, Linda, dear!"

"She did. I just know she did! Her hair uncombed— and her dress all rumpled. Imagine going out to tea like that—after keeping everyone waiting for hours!"

Sarah was back in the kitchen before she knew it. She stared at her reflection in the mirror, biting hard on her forefinger. That way you couldn't feel the inside hurt so much. A moment, then Sarah knew what she was going to do. The side door offered a way of escape. It opened almost noiselessly, and it closed gently behind her. She ducked as she raced past the window.

You would have expected that Hyacinthe would behave now that she was headed for home. It was no such thing! The minute Sarah climbed onto her back she began acting up—rearing, prancing, snorting. Where the lane joined the road Sarah slid from the mare's back. Then she stood helplessly in the middle of the dusty road, turning, hanging onto the halter rope while Hyacinthe pranced round and round her.

"Please, *please,* Hyacinthe!" she begged.

She was shaking. Her eyes were blurred with heat and unshed tears. Suddenly she saw someone running across the field—and jump the fence—and the next moment a strong hand closed over hers.

"Behave yourself, Hyacinthe," said a man's voice firmly. Herbie Gerrick!

In a moment he had Hyacinthe snubbed fast to a telephone post. Let her try any of her rearing tricks now! In another moment Herbie drew Sarah down to sit on a gate pole beside him.

"There, there!" He patted her shoulder. "You're safe now. But you go ahead and cry if you want to. I'll never tell."

"I can't," whispered Sarah, still shaking all over.

"Well, then, could you tell me what this is all about? It might help."

Sarah told. About the magic twenty-fifth that turned out to be no magic at all. About hurrying home from school—

and the chores and about riding because she was so late
She told how lovely Linda wa —and about the beautiful
dolls—and the cream puffs—

"But I don't see—" began Herbie, sounding puzzled. "If
your n w r nd is l ely and l wh t *happ d*

"She— She doesn't ant to see me ever again. I smel
she says. She says I m awful. She laughed at my riding.
Herbie, what does *crude* mean?'

"Did she use the word?

Sarah nodded in numb misery.

"Crude, are you? W ll, I'd like to march right up to the
young Miss High-and Mighty and tell her who is crude. For
two cents I'd do it this minute! Imagine telling a guest
that!"

Sarah giggled weakly, and leaned her head against his
dusty shirtsleeve. It felt wonderful to have him sticking
up for her like this

"I don't have two cents. But Herbie you go ahead and
marry Kathleen if you want to.'

"Tha ks Sarah," he said gra ely Thanks a lot."

CHAPTER 7

June Picnic

THE SCOTT FAMILY was sitting around the supper table when Sarah walked in quietly. Her glance went around the circle slowly. Then she looked only at Father.

"Well!" he said gravely. "So you're back—and all in one piece, I see."

She nodded, but she wasn't sure it was entirely true. Inside she felt as if she had been broken into a thousand bits and pieces.

"Where's Hyacinthe?"

"In the pasture, Father."

"And what have you to say for yourself, young lady?"

"About—about Hyacinthe?"

"About your taking her without permission."

"I—I rode her at home—sometimes. And you saw me. And you didn't ever tell me I wasn't ever to. And—"

"Well, listen carefully now, because I'm telling you—"

But Mother interrupted. "Sarah, come here."

She moved closer, not looking at anyone. Mother's arm went around her.

"What happened? *Something's* happened. You went to see Linda. What is she like?"

Sarah stared down at the flowered oilcloth on the table.

"She has blond hair and blue eyes. Just like in a storybook. And—" Her voice trailed away.

She had told Herbie all the things she heard Linda say about her. But somehow she couldn't repeat it to Mother and the others.

"And?"

"I—I'm tired. Mayn't I go to bed?"

"I suppose so. But take a good wash—and don't forget to pray."

She didn't forget. But all the same, she didn't pray that night. What was the use? She had prayed *and prayed* for a special friend. And Linda came. But Linda said those horrid words— Over and over they came back to torture Sarah. *She's awful. She's crude. I don't want to see her, not ever again. She smells. Horsey—* Sarah rolled over and pulled the pillow up to shut her ears against the sound. It did no good.

"Not asleep *yet?*" said Kathleen when she came to bed. "Look here, Kiddo. What did happen over at Miss Bolton's? Can't you tell me?"

A slight shake of the head was her only answer.

"Should I call Mother? You ought to speak to someone."

"I did."

"To whom?"

"Herbie. He brought me home. In the runabout, right up to the pasture gate. And he turned Hyacinthe in there. She was naughty, Kathleen. I couldn't manage her. So Herbie came running from the field. He just left his team and came running. He's nice, Kathleen."

"Well! And well, well!" said Kathleen softly, and she laughed a bit. "So you like him now?"

"And I told him he could marry you if he wanted to."

'You d dn't!" Kathleen sounded shocked and pleased and a b t w rried "Oh, Sarah! How could you!"

"Easy I j t did."

Kathleen had leaned over to pat her cheek. Her hand jerked backward. "Child! You're burning up!" She tiptoed oward the door. "I'll be right back, Chickie."

Sarah had begun shivering Funny. Her body couldn't seem to make up ts mind if it was too hot or too cold It was too *something*. Her head ached. In her chest there was this chunk of ice, big as two fists. And she was shaking, shaking— But her face was hot as the top of a stove.

Kathleen ame tiptoeing back. All the rest of the family was asleep by now. Gently Kathleen swabbed Sarah's face with a cool wet cloth. Suddenly the chunk of ice began melting And suddenly Sarah was in Kathleen's arms and Kathleen was rocking back and forth on the bed, listening to her sobbing out her story, and comforting her

"You re nice " whispered Sarah at last, and with a sigh she went o sleep

Kathl en must have told the others. For a few days nobody men ioned the magic twenty-fifth of May nor scolded her for taking Hya inthe Whenever Sarah walked to school alone she went west for a mile and a half before turning south That way she needn t pass Aunt Jane's place. At home she played with Ginger and Spencer, and she rounded up the cows, and gathered egg, and took the goslings for their daily swim. They were ge ting bigger and sassier and more untidy-looking every day. They *needed* the bath.

Time slid past This was June now. There were dande lions and buttercups in the wayside grasses, and m llions of roses in the wayside hedges. On the way to s hoo Sarah and Robbie found a meadowlark's nest— Spring was just the same as always.

But Mother was worried. She came to sit beside Sarah on the porchstep one day.

'Wouldn't you like to drop in to see Linda today?" she asked

' No, thank you, Mother."

"I ll bake a cake—and you may help me decorate it, and—"

'No, thank you just the same." Sarah went on tickling Spencer's ears, and squinting at the pond where about five hundred frogs were croaking.

"Why not, dear?"

Slowly and distinctly Sarah said the words aloud. ' I *hate* Linda Bolton."

"Oh, darling! Oh, poor lamb!"

"*Linda?*" scoffed Sarah "*She's* not poor. You shoulda seen her books and the dolls—spiffy as anything, in silks and feathers and laces."

"I wasn't thinking about Linda," said Mother quietly. It was the kind of quietness that sends a strange stabby feeling through you. "I do feel sorry for her—and so should you. In your heart I'm sure you do feel sorry Try to imagine what it's like not to be able to run, or climb trees, or ride— '

"*You call that riding?*" *That's what Linda said. Serves her right that she can't run*, thought Sarah stubbornly. *Serves her just exactly right!*

Mother was still talking. "I feel most sorry for my little girl. Harboring hatred is such a sad and useless and harmful thing. And it's the one who does the hating who is harmed.'

Sarah kept silent. But Spencer knew something was wrong. He must have felt the sadness that came to him through the hands that were stroking his head. He licked Sarah's face and crowded close.

In the next days Sarah told herself firmly for about the fifty-seventh time that everything was just exactly the way it always was. The wind in the grasses—and the racing cloud shadows—and the oriole call—and the wren s warbling— Just the same. Rattling to school in the old buggy—playing softball on the schoolyard at recess—studying for the exams with the windows open so the breezes rustled the pages. This was June.

June was examination time. And after that came picnic day!

"Tomorrow's picnic day—picnic day—picnic day" chanted Sarah, leaning against the kitchen table and munching a hot crisp doughnut. Mother was frying a batch For tomorrow And Kathleen was icing the cake. *For tomorrow.* Sarah held out her half-eaten doughnut. Obligingly Kathleen dropped a blob of icing on it. Sarah munched happily and thought of the new dress she was going to wear to the picnic.

"It's going to rain," predicted Father.

"Oh, no!" protested Sarah. "Father, you musn't *say* it!"

"My saying it won't make it rain. But the sky has a threatening look."

And Father was right. When Sarah awoke next morning she heard rain pattering on the roof. She gave one dismayed glance out the window, and burrowed under her bedclothes again.

"Get up, sleepyhead," called Kathleen. "Are you forgetting? Picnic day!"

"It's raining," said Sarah grumpily.

'Rain before seven stops before eleven,' recited Kathleen. "Don't you remember? We usually have rain in the forenoon of picnic day."

Sarah sat straight up. That was true! It was true as true! Last year—and the year before that—it rained in the forenoon. She had to hurry! She and Robbie had to be in school this morning, rain or no rain. Miss Halliday was going to hand out report cards. Oh, she hoped she'd passed! Besides, the school was to have its final rehearsal for the picnic program. Sarah was going to be the Spirit of Knowledge in a play. If only the sky would clear!

Most of the forenoon was showery. At recess time Braeburn pupils stood in forlorn huddles staring skyward, as if their combined gaze could tear holes in the scudding clouds. The bell called for the final school period. Gloomily they took their seats.

"Cheer up," advised Miss Halliday. "If it should continue to shower, the board said we would have a party right in school—an indoor picnic!"

They looked at her in silent pity. It must be dreadful to be a grown-up if a party in an everydayish schoolroom could seem just as pleasant to you as a *picnic*.

The report cards turned their thoughts to other miseries —or joys. Most of them had passed their grades, though. Sarah even squeaked by in geography. Goody! She never could remember which countries exported what to which other countries— In the other subjects, except spelling, she had over eighty. Spelling—well sixty-five was pretty good for Sarah Naomi Scott. And that moment the first watery gleam of sunshine actually broke through the shredding clouds. The faces of Braeburn pupils took on more

and more radiance to match the ou doors. The final rehearsal of the program was zestful. Robbie was a tramp in
a funny dialogue. He made an awfully good tramp.

Then, after gulping their lunches, they all left for the
picnic grounds.

They were in a meadow about a mile west of the school.
The grass was drying quickly in the wind and sun. There
were poplar groves for shade, and today the flag waved
proudly from a pole. There was a plank platform for the
performers, and plank seats for the audience. There were
long picnic tables for the eats. Mothers and big sisters
came bringing pails and boxes and roasters full of things.
It wasn't safe to pass the tables too early. You got too hun
gry, and a lot was to happen before the feasting could begin.

Still it was fascinating to watch the preparations. Father
and Mr. Thatcher and Mr. Siddons were the ice-cream mak-
ers. Actually the mothers mixed the farm cream and the
milk and eggs and the sugar and vanilla. But the men filled
gunny sacks with cakes of ice and pounded them to slivers.
Pretty soon the freezers were squeaking comfortably, while
the men squatted in the shade, turning the handles—paus-
ing to test the ice cream—and going back to turning handles again.

More and more people gathered all the while. Most of
them drove cars, but there were some buggies, and even a
wagon. Braeburn picnics were famous. People came from
miles around, people who didn t belong to the district and
never had. All of Braeburn was there, of course—all but
Aunt Jane and Linda. And no one missed them, thought
Sarah with a queer little thrill of pity.

Everyone said later that the program was just wonderful.

The eighth grade girls sang a sad and lovely song, all about their school days now being past and gone—and they were bidding everyone a sweet farewell. The Spirit of Knowledge did all right too. It wasn't her fault that the wind kept blowing her cheesecloth overskirt into her mouth right in the middle of her longest speech. The people liked it fine. They laughed almost as hard as they did at Robbie. Sarah didn't mind. They *clapped* as hard for her too.

After that came the races, just to get everyone good and hungry. Three-legged races, sack races, wheelbarrow races, thread-the-needle races— The men had to run to the ladies carrying needles for the ladies to thread, and then run back to the starting place again. Herbie and Kathleen won that one, and everyone clapped and laughed again.

When the time came for lunch, Braeburn pupils got the first call. This was their special day.

"Well, Sarah!" said Sister Hammond. Soft yet solid she leaned across Sarah to place another plateful of sandwiches on the table. Salmon and lettuce, Sarah's favorite.

"Brother Hammond and I dropped in on Miss Jane Bolton and her niece the other night. It seems such a pity the way that girl has to sit still all day. You are so active I know you will feel especially sympathetic. Miss Bolton told me you came the very day Linda arrived. That was thoughtful of— Yes, Mrs. Thatcher. I saw her. She seems very patient, considering— A most ladylike and mature girl she is, too. Beautiful manners. Have a sandwich, Sarah dear?"

"N-no, thank you. I better not."

"Another helping of ice cream then?"

"No, thank you. I think I've had enough."

It was a good thing others were finishing too. And just then someone called, "Play ball!" Sarah could escape.

John Siddons' wrist was dislocated, so Sarah was left fielder in his place. Braeburn school was to play against outsiders. Robbie pitched for the school. Stuart for the outsiders. It wasn't fair. Sarah wouldn't know for which side to cheer.

People who weren't playing sat on the grass watching the game and chatting. Fathers, mothers, babies, everybody. Sarah had a lonesome job. But she had a beautiful moment when she caught a long fly—and zipped it across to Robbie. The bases were loaded! One-two-three—and out! That's the way the play went.

Yaaaay Braeburn!

Sarah grinned at Stuart as she trotted past. He shook his head at her. "You're too smart, sister. Just for that I'll make it rough fo you. See if I don't."

He didn't. She actually got to second base. Braeburn won—thirteen to eleven—and the outsiders challenged the school to another game.

But it was choring time. Most of the grown-ups and the children left for home.

School was over for the year.

CHAPTER 8

First of July

IT WAS THE DAY after the Braeburn picnic. Sarah wondered what could be the matter with Kathleen. She seemed so jumpy today. Not bossy, just jumpy.

Of course, this was a busy day on the Scott farm. Because, tomorrow was the First of July, which is Canada's birthday. Always on that day the whole Scott family went fishing. Someone else did the milking for them. The Scotts couldn't wait. When the eastern sky was barely streaky with light they would be up, out of bed. Before the sun popped over the Heathe birches, they would be on their way. A thirty-mile ride in a buggy is pretty far. You have to have an early start.

Susan Gerrick thought driving a buggy was an awfully slowpoky way of going to a picnic. But Mother explained to Sarah that you didn't go *to* a family outing. You went *on* one. The picnic began the minute everyone was settled in the buggy, and Father or Stuart gathered up the reins to cluck to Prince and Captain.

Maybe it began earlier than that. Sarah thought it did. Like right *now*—helping to pack the picnic things in a big cardboard box. Salt and flour, lard and eggs, tin plates and cups, old knives and forks and spoons— Mother was sticking the big long-handled frypan into a gunny sack and the old waffle iron into another. There'd be hot waffles on the shore of Loon Lake, with the water all silver and purply with mist, and maybe the loons far across the lake sending out their quivery laughter— Nothing can be nicer than that.

Unless it's going out with the rowboat after breakfast, quiet, not speaking, just sort of gliding into the mist— Or maybe coming back to shore with a mess of fish, and frying them over the fire, and sitting around and talking, just *family.*

Sometimes you couldn't help wondering— Where was Keith? And did he ever think about the family fishing trips? Did they have them when he was at home? Sarah thought they must have. The Scotts did the same things year by year. That was one of the nice things about belonging to this family.

The Gerricks had a car—but they never went for an outing at all. They said they couldn't afford to take the *time.* Sarah sighed with happiness. She was a Scott not a Gerrick.

She was too polite though to mention the picnic to Herbie when he dropped in that evening. For some reason, Herbie looked a bit jumpy too. He had supper with the family—but he spoke hardly at all. Kathleen wasn't helping. She kept getting up to see if someone was missing something. Did Father want more coffee? No? What about Stuart then?

Stuart was grinning. So was Robbie. Every little bit Sarah saw Robbie give Stuart a nudge with his elbow— which was no way to behave at the table. Then they almost split their faces again grinning. Mother shook her head at them once, but Father had a little secret smile on his face too. Only Herbie was serious, and he was getting redder by the minute. Nobody was behaving the usual way. What was the *matter* with everybody?

After supper Herbie and Kathleen went straight to the parlor. Just up and went! For some singing, maybe! Father and Mother were going too— But when Sarah tried to follow, Father whispered, 'Not now, Princess." And he shut the door in her face.

Sarah could only stare at the tableful of dirty dishes. Did this mean she had to do them all *alone?*

"Get a wiggle on, small-fry," spoke up Stuart. If you get 'em stacked in ten minutes I'll dry 'em for you. Robbie, you can lend a hand too'

'Oh, goody! Thank you Stuart." It was fun to do dishes with Stuart. He always had so many jokes to tell.

But today he said, "Don't thank me. I want to stick around anyhow—to see Herbie and Kathleen when they come out of there."

"Why?"

The boys hooted aloud this time, and they called her Miss Innocence.

"They're *engaged,* that's why. Happened after the picnic, I guess. And Herbie's asking Father and Mother if it's all right—and making wedding plans—things like that."

"Pooh!" said Sarah. "I knew about *that!* I told Herbie he could marry her if he wanted to."

"You didn't!"

"I did so!"

"When? You tell me when." said Robbie.

But Sarah buttoned up her mouth. She wasn't going to talk about the magic twenty-fifth of May even if they'd think she was fibbing.

Engaged. That meant Kathleen would be Mrs. Herbie Gerrick. And Gerricks didn't believe in outings. Maybe she would never have time again for a family picnic. Poor Kathleen!

It was a strange evening. When the parlor door opened there was a lot of teasing laughter. Herbie's face was as red as ever, but he laughed as much as anyone now. He went out to the runabout and brought a five-pound box of candy for Kathleen. It was tied with an enormous red satin bow. But suddenly he placed a smaller box into Sarah's hands. A whole pound of chocolates! Hers had a blue ribbon.

"What for?" she blurted, not believing it.

Laughing, Kathleen hugged and kissed her. "Herbie insists he might never have had the courage to speak up if it hadn't been for you." Then she whispered, "You really like him now, don't you?"

Sarah nodded soberly. "But not on account of the candy," she whispered back. "He's nice."

"I know." Kathleen squeezed her hand.

Later Mother had an idea. "Should I ask Susan if she would care to come with us tomorrow?"

"Oh, no!"

"Why, Sarah! You surprise me. Susan is your friend, isn't she? Why don't you want her to come along?"

"She always wants to whisper. It tickles."

And it did seem sort of silly. Sarah could imagine Susan sitting beside her on the sand. They two all alone, with only the gulls nearby. But still she would whisper. The main thing though was that Sarah liked to go boating with her brothers and with Father. That's the way she did every

year. If Susan came she'd have to play little girl games most of the day.

There was one change this year. Kathleen stayed home to milk the cows in the morning. Then she and Herbie were coming in the runabout, and they promised to be on time for breakfast. They better! They were to bring a lot of food—butter, and milk, and things that needed to be kept cold.

The outings always began sort of quietly. Prince and Captain's hooves beat a quiet clip-clop rhythm on the damp dirt road. Pretty soon they turned off the main road to follow a grassy trail, with bushes crowding in on both sides. You leaned back to watch the pink and gold light sort of shivering from cloud to cloud. You watched the day awaken. Birds hopped from branch to branch right to the tips of the trees. They bowed, and they spread their wings, fluttering them, shaking the sleepiness out of every feather. Then they sang. How they sang!

Smiling, Father lifted his cap. "Thanks for the reminder, all you feathered folk," he called out. "Time for us Scotts to raise our voices."

They did. They sang, "Oh, Thou in whose presence my soul takes delight. . . ." And, "Fairest Lord Jesus. . . ." And, "God is love, His mercy brightens all the paths in which we rove. . . ." This one had a lot of fancy swooping notes. Sarah loved it.

They trotted past the place where a forest fire raced through over a year ago. Last year it was black, black. Now the ugly gash was all grown over with lovely purple fireweed. Father said it reminded him of the way God's grace can make something lovely out of a sinner's life. And Mother began singing, "Marvelous grace of our loving

Lord. . . ." They passed the rocky hill that looked like a castle—and Father thought of "A Mighty Fortress Is Our God."

Sarah thought, *Almost there now.*

Just when they began looping through the hills down toward the lake there was a croaking whistle behind them. Prince and Captain were so startled that they leaped sideway out of the rutted trail. Herbie and Kathleen came speeding past, laughing and waving.

"That young man had better tend strictly to his driving," said Father. "He has precious cargo aboard." Then in a low voice he said, "Well, Mother?"

Sarah sat between her parents. She couldn't help overhearing. Father's "Well, Mother?" seemed to be asking, "How do you feel about the engagement? Will they be happy? Will he be good to her?"

Mother said softly, "I have no greater joy than to hear that my children walk in the truth. That is my dearest desire for them. Not ease, nor riches. Not even happiness— as we humans count happiness. But oh, that all of them would choose to serve God with all their hearts."

"Amen!" said Father. His voice, deep and solemn the way it sometimes was in church, sent a funny thrill down Sarah's back.

That minute the horses broke into a spanking trot. The buggy whirled around the last bend. There was the beach with the lapping waves. There was the boatkeeper's house perched high on a hill. There was Herbie's car, with Herbie lighting a fire nearby, and Kathleen mixing the waffle batter. Hooray! Picnic day!

It was a long and lazy kind of day. And that seemed sort of funny. At home Father and Mother were always working, working. It was strange to see them just sitting around. Funny—but nice. Trolling—or just drifting along in the rowboat—or padding barefooted over the sand, looking for shells, or building sand castles. By noon the waffles were nothing but a fragrant memory, Father said. There was plenty of room for baked ham, and potato salad, and pickles and pie. It was the same at supper time. But then they ate crisp fried fish.

"We might as well make a day of it," Father said when Mother wondered if *this year* they ought to start for home a bit earlier.

Just as the sun was setting they all went for a last boat ride. Because this was Canada's birthday they sang, "O Canada!" and "The Maple Leaf Forever!" There's nothing nicer than singing on a still lake just when the sun is sinking behind the spruce trees.

They made a bonfire on the shore then. And as Father always did, he led devotions. He read that bit about Abraham seeking " a country and a city which hath foundations, whose builder and maker is God." Mother said they should sing, "Heaven Is My Home," and they did.

Then in the soft dark and the silence they went home.

Sarah wondered why it was that she often felt saddest just when she had been the happiest. She sat between Father and Mother again going home. They thought she was asleep. Mother drew the coarse wool blanket up and tucked it under her chin. They talked in low voices. But Sarah was thinking—thinking—

Something disturbing happened after supper today. Stuart and Robbie were out in the boat for a last ride. But Father and Herbie were helping Mother and Kathleen wash the dishes and pack the things, and clean up the camping place. And they talked.

Sarah had curled up in a little hollow near the fire. She couldn't help hearing. And nobody cared if she did. It wasn't a secret.

An evangelist was coming to Braeburn church—coming all the way from Scotland! Brother Murchison, they called him. What was an *evangelist*? Sarah wasn't sure she knew. So why did her heart have to go thumping the funny way it did?

There'd be meetings. Herbie and Kathleen were church members, but it didn't seem to Sarah that they were as happy as Father and Mother about Brother Murchison. Herbie thought July wasn't really a suitable time. There was all the haying to be done. It wasn't going to be easy to unhitch the workhorses early enough in order to rush through chores, so as to be in church on time every evening for two weeks. That was expecting an awful lot, it seemed to him. It was different for those who had tractors.

Father said, "It depends on how you look at it. Which is more important—seeing hay cured, or seeing souls saved? Braeburn needs a revival, and please God, we're going to have one!"

"You're right. Of course, you're right, Mr. Scott. I didn't mean—" said Herbie. "But I *was* hoping to have a bit of free time this summer to work at the house on my place—so it will be ready for Kathleen by fall."

Maybe that was what made her feel so sad, thought Sarah as she listened now to the steady beat of Prince's and Captain's hooves. *Going home—We're going home*—they seemed to be saying. But pretty soon Kathleen would have a home of her own. Things would never be the same again.

CHAPTER 9

Summertime

SUMMER HOLIDAYS— A busy time, a lazy time. This was an odd thing: Some of the busiest times actually seemed to be the laziest—and some of the laziest times really were the busiest. At least, that's the way it seemed to Sarah.

The grown-ups all were busy all the time, of course. Out on the fields there was the summer fallow to crisscross with the disc and the harrow. In order to kill the weeds. After that came haying time. After that would come the cutting of grain. And the stooking.* And the threshing— There was so much to do that Robbie sometimes got counted in with the grown-ups. He was thirteen now.

Mother and Kathleen did the gardening. And this summer they were quilting thick wool blankets, and stuffing new pillows, making things for Kathleen's new home. And always, morning and evening, there were the chores waiting to be done.

The job Robbie didn't like was weeding the garden. That was women's work he said, grumbling a bit. It wasn't so bad, thought Sarah. They fooled around a lot, she and Robbie. Sometimes they would tell made-up stories to each other, laughing like anything. Sometimes they raced each other along the rows of vegetables, chopping and pulling at

*Bundling the grain in shocks.

weeds. When the ground was dry, they hitched old Wally to a sled with two barrels sitting on it. They led him down to the creek, and dipped up the water by pailfuls, not hurrying because it was so cool here on a sizzling hot day. Overhead, millions of leaves would be clapping their hands softly. Below, the water gurgled and rippled—and you wished you could stay here forever. But the garden was wilting in the sun.

Climbing the hill again, the water slip-slapped in the barrels. *Coming—coming—water's coming*—they seemed to be saying.

Pretty soon the cool stream would be moving along the shallow trenches between rows of beets and carrots, onions, peas and corn, and sinking into the thirsty ground. And in minutes you'd see all the plants standing crisp and tall once more. It was a proud thing to watch.

Those were the lazy days.

The busy times came when Sarah lay curled up in her private place under the crab apple tree. That was when she thought, and thought—until her head seemed to be spinning.

She thought about Kathleen and Herbie—and about the wedding that was coming in fall. She had never been to a wedding. Never! It would be exciting—and strange. It would seem *very* strange to have a brother-in-law. Sometimes she was sorry she had ever told Herbie he could be. And Susan would be Kathleen's sister-in-law. She *hoped* Kathleen wouldn't go and love Susan best!

She thought of Linda. She didn't want to, but she did. Words like *crude* and *smelly* and *horrid* sort of spun round and round in her head, and made her feel hot and choky.

She thought of Brother Murchison. He was coming

soon now. Father and Mother were talking and praying about it more and more every day. But nobody else did much. Not in the Scott home. Sarah wondered a bit about that. When at the table Father mentioned the meetings, Robbie got red in the face, Stuart seemed not to hear, Kathleen mostly changed the subject. Practically all she talked about these days was the cupboards Herbie was building in his house, and the kind of curtains she meant to sew for the windows, and about wallpaper samples, and paint colors. Things like that.

Sarah couldn't help wondering. Did their hearts all go thumpity-thump the way hers did whenever she heard about the meetings? And why was that? What was *getting saved?*

For a long time she wanted to ask Kathleen. She wanted to—she was afraid to. One evening she just did.

"It's—it's giving your heart to the Lord Jesus."

"Did you?"

Kathleen said, "Y-yes," as if she wasn't very sure, or as if she was thinking about something else. Then she said it again. "Yes!"

Sarah whispered the next question. "Aren't you—when you're saved—aren't you scared of God anymore?"

Kathleen looked up from her wallpaper samples. She came to sit on the bed beside Sarah then. But Sarah was examining her toes as if she had never seen anything so curious before.

"Sarah, are *you* afraid of God?"

Sarah nodded. "Some."

"Oh, you don't have to be! Tell Him about it, honey. Ask Him to clean your heart, for Jesus' sake."

"Is that the same as getting *saved?*"

"Yes. That's another name for it. All of us are sinners. We're born that way. And when we *know* we have sin in our hearts, we're afraid of Him. But we needn't be. Jesus died in our stead, Sarah."

"When did you?"

"Get saved? When I was fourteen."

Fourteen! Sarah took a deep breath. Why, then there was lots of time. Suddenly she felt happier than she had in weeks. *Fourteen.* There was no hurry at all.

"Sarah—" Kathleen tried to put her arm around Sarah, but she wriggled free.

"I'm awfully sleepy," she said, making her voice sound sort of fuzzy.

Kathleen sighed. "OK. Good night, then. You'll not forget to pray, will you?" she said. "Honey?"

"No, I won't," Sarah grunted into her pillow.

She didn't forget—and she didn't pray.

She almost never prayed now. She was getting to be dreadfully wicked, she thought a trifle proudly. A real lost lamb. She pretended to be sleepy when she wasn't. That was a lie. She said she was *some* afraid of God. Even that was a bit of a lie. She was awfully *terribly* afraid! That's why she didn't pray. She didn't dare to. Practically the only time she did pray now was when she was more scared not to—like during a thunderstorm.

But all the same, she didn't want to get saved. Not now. When she was fourteen. Maybe.

The next morning the sun rose just the same as always. Sarah was almost surprised. God hadn't punished her for being wicked. The sunlight was the same. And Spencer loved her just as much. And the dew lay on the grass and shrubs all around.

Because of it Father and Stuart couldn't go to the field as early as usual. They were stacking hay. It had to be dry. So this morning they helped with chores. Stuart teased her while she was looking for stray eggs in the hayloft. This evening the loft would hold a mountain of hay.

When she came nimbly down the ladder Father said, "Well! Who's so spry this morning? Care to help me saddle Hyacinthe? This seems the right day to give her—and you—some riding pointers."

That's the way the day began.

In the afternoon, when all the little breezes were taking a nap, and the sun just shone and shone, Mother called Sarah to help her take some refreshments out to the field.

"But wear your straw hat," she warned. "This heat is so oppressive."

Mother had put on her sunbonnet and her gardening mitts. They were made of a pair of stockings, and they came right up to her sleeve. It would be dreadful for a lady to get brown from the sun. But a little girl could. Sarah was glad she was no lady. She had to wear sandals, though. Tufts of prairie grass can really cut your bare feet. But her legs were bare and brown—as brown as the hand that carried the gallon pailful of cold, cold buttermilk.

On the far end of the meadow Stuart was cutting the grass, driving Prince and Captain around and around in tightening ovals. Clickety-clack, clickety-clack went the mower knives. The green grass lay in flat neat rows. Sarah thought the smell of drying grass was one of the nicest smells in the world.

Stuart saw them coming. He waved his hat. Then he tethered the team to the nearest bush and came striding across the field. Father was tossing great forkfuls of hay onto a rack. Robbie was up there forking it into place and tramping it down.

In the shade of the rack Mother unpacked the basket. There were fresh currant buns, and slices of cheese, and butter, and the buttermilk. Father and the boys took off their hats. Father had a red circle around his forehead, from the heat and the sweat, and his hair was all wet and curly.

"Let's ask the blessing," he said.

Then they ate, and they talked— About how many loads of hay there'd be on the field. The loft could never, never hold it all, said Father! God had been very good to them. They'd make a long stack right here in the meadow.

"Will you finish the haying before Sunday?" said Mother.

"I hope so. I'm sure we can if the weather holds."

Sunday. Brother Murchison would be here by then.

That Saturday, for the first time since Sarah could remember, there was no singing in the Scott home. Storm clouds were coming closer, closer— And there were *loads* of hay left on the field, unstacked. Father borrowed a rack from the Heathes. Kathleen and Mother drove one rack, Stuart and Robbie the other. Father and Sarah stayed at home. Theirs was the most exciting job of all.

The one end of the loft was a sort of drop door on hinges, though it was closed fast most of the year. Up under the barn ridge hung a big pulley wheel around which went a long heavy rope. Captain and Prince were hitched to the other end of the rope today.

Father let down the drop door so it became a platform. The opening looked like a gaping mouth, a giant mouth, just waiting to swallow you whole. When a load of hay

pulled up to the barn, they all worked fast, forking the hay from the rack onto the platform. Sarah stood near the horses' heads, talking to them. But she kept watching Father too. When the platform was loaded he raised his arm and shouted, "All right!"

Sarah clucked at the horses to pull the rope. "Whoa, not so fast. There! That's better."

You had to move slowly, steadily. This was important. Oh, whee! Oh, wow! The platform was tilting, up, and up— *Gulp*. The giant had swallowed the hay!

"Whoa!" shouted Father.

Another load was safe in the loft. Sarah led the horses back to where they started from, so the hungry mouth could be opened for another swallow.

And away rattled the rack, going for another load. But the clouds were boiling up higher and higher—

"The last of the hay!" called Stuart, driving up just as Mother and Kathleen were pitching the last of their load.

"Well done!" shouted Father.

A minute later a raindrop hit Sarah's nose. "Run, Princess! Run for the house!" called Father. "Robbie, you take charge of the team."

Sarah ran. But the clouds won the race. They simply opened up, and down came frothy rivers that slicked your clothes and pasted your eyes shut, and made foamy brown seas of the whole yard. That minute there was a terrifying clap of thunder. Sarah jerked so, she slipped and fell on her face. Then she was up and running like the wettest rabbit you ever saw, while the thunder rattled and rolled overhead.

Dripping wet, her heart thumping, she stood at the kitchen window then. Through sheets of rain she saw Stuart running with Prince and Captain, to close up the loft in a hurry. Robbie was helping Father to unhitch the other team. Mother and Kathleen were shooing the drowning chicks and the mother hens into the chicken house. Everyone soaking wet, everyone running as fast as the rain and the wind let them.

Supper was late. Because of the soaking they'd all had, they took their baths first. And it seemed even later than it was. The growling storm clouds darkened the kitchen. It seemed strange to be eating by lamplight in summer.

The wet hair and clean shirts and things smelled homey. The lamp on the table threw a warm glow over the faces and the food. But Sarah had no appetite.

Oh, if only the thundering would stop. She thought, *God must be terribly angry. Maybe because of me.*

Then she remembered that tomorrow was Sunday, and that Brother Murchison was going to be there. But if the rain kept coming, maybe *this* time the Scotts would stay at home!

The rain continued. All night, and all morning. Not quite so hard, but it was more than a drizzle. The Scotts went to church just the same.

"We're none of us made of sugar," said Mother firmly. "We can wrap blankets around us. The people who have nothing but cars for traveling will hardly be able to leave home today. It would be a shame if Brother Murchison had no audience at all."

He had seventeen listeners. He preached as if there were about two hundred there! Father said later that it was a very powerful sermon.

CHAPTER 10

Sarah's Rebellion

THERE WERE SO FEW at the service this first rainy Sunday morning that Brother Murchison shook hands with *everybody*.

He was tall, and his eyes were sharp under their bushy brows. Sarah was afraid of him. He took her hand, and he stooped, smiling a little.

"Well, lassie, have ye gi'en your hairt to the Lord Jesus yet?"

Nobody was listening. Nobody would ever know.

"Yes," whispered Sarah.

"God bless ye. Of such is the kingdom of heaven," said Brother Murchison, placing his big hand gently on her head.

Sarah wasn't sorry she had told a lie. Now Brother Murchison wouldn't bother her again, she thought. She never expected him to come and visit at their house—on such a rainy day!

Mother invited him—and he came.

"Och, 'tis nothing but a drizzle," he said when Mother worried a bit about his getting damp. "Gude for the lungs, moist air, Sister Scott."

And at the dinner table he had to go and tell everybody that he was so happy to hear that Sarah was a child of God!

They were too polite—maybe too *surprised*—to say anything *then*. Later Kathleen looked at her searchingly and asked, "When did it happen, Honey?" And Robbie caught her when she was gathering eggs. He closed the door of the chicken house, and came close. "You're smart!" he whispered. "I wish I'd thought of it."

But Mother came to her room while she was getting ready for evening service. She sat on the bed, looking grave. And she talked. Sarah pretended not to be listening.

"Would you comb my hair, Mother?" she said. And, "Please tie my sash, Mother. You make such lovely bows. Susan's always are crooked as anything and all squashed up."

"Sarah, I want you to listen carefully. Lying to God is a very dangerous thing. You cannot fool Him. I hope you'll think seriously about this. Oh, my darling! My last little baby. What has happened to you this past while?"

Mother had tears in her eyes. Sarah looked away quickly to stare out the window. Finally Mother went away.

That was the way things began. From that day Sarah was a naughty girl. Sometimes she felt miserable about it. Sometimes she was proud of her naughtiness. Always, it seemed, she couldn't help herself. Someone was *making* her do these things. During the evening meetings she giggled, and she whispered funny things to make other girls giggle too.

And then one day she did the very worst thing of all.

Mother and Kathleen went to Blakely in the forenoon. Sarah was supposed to stay in her room for punishment because she sassed back that morning. But as soon as Mother was away she ran out, and she bridled Captain, and she rode over to Aunt Jane's place. She knew Aunt Jane was away. She had seen the car leave the yard. But Linda was at the open window.

She looked surprised. Then her face turned almost friendly, and just a bit timid.

"Hello, Sarah," she called, leaning out. "I'm sorry Aunt Jane isn't at home. And—and I'm sorry I was so rude the last ti—"

"Rude—crude," yelled Sarah. And she stuck out her tongue.

Then she made Captain turn in circles and figure eights. She stood on his back. She lay down flat on it. She did every single trick she had ever practiced with him. All the time she was saying, *See? You can't do this—and this—and this. You're a cripple! You'll never be able to do any fun thing, ever again.*

She never spoke a word, but that was what she was saying all the same. And Linda understood. Her head lay on the sill, and her shoulders were shaking. Sarah felt just a teeny bit sorry then. But she turned Captain, and she clattered home, and turned him into the pasture, and scampered up to her room.

Mother will never find out, she thought.

But Linda must have told Aunt Jane. And that afternoon something happened—the thing that nobody thought would *ever* happen again. Miss Jane Bolton drove in her sedan right up to the Scott lane, and stopped in front of the garden gate.

Sarah who was in the kitchen heard her mother whisper, "Oh, I thank thee, Lord!"

And now she was running to the door— Mother *running!*

Like a little girl! And she was calling, "Jane! Jane! Oh my dear Jane! You've come!"

But Sarah stayed right where she was, and her heart went thump thump thump.

She heard Miss Bolton say, "You seem to labor under a slight misapprehension, Sheila Scott. Where is Sarah? I've come to see her—to give her a piece of my mind. Believe me, she richly deserves it."

Sarah wasn't standing still now. On tiptoes she raced to her parents' bedroom. She opened the window, and wriggled through, and dropped to the ground, and closed the window, and ducked low to scuttle across the garden, from cranberry bush to gooseberry bush till she could dive into her private place under the crab apple tree. Spencer wanted to come too. She gave him a hard kick with her bare heel. "Get away! Go!" she whispered sharply. He looked reproachfully at her, and then walked gravely away. Sarah curled up, her heart hammering like anything.

She knew what Miss Bolton was talking about—

She wished—oh, *how* she *wished* that Brother Murchison had never, never come to Braeburn church. That was when her troubles had begun. Ever since she had told him the lie about being a child of God she'd been getting naughtier and naughtier. And today she did this awful thing to Linda. Now Aunt Jane was blabbing to Mother.

Sarah waited, her heart thudding slowly. For a long time nothing happened. Aunt Jane's car had gone snorting away. *Still* nothing happened. Then she heard something rustle.

A voice called, "Sarah! Sarah Naomi, where are you?" Father!

"Sarah, come out at once!"

She had never been so frightened of him before in all her life. He looked ashamed, ashamed of *her*. And he looked sad and very stern. Standing there between the gooseberry bushes he got her to tell exactly what happened this morning.

"Sarah, we have tried everything, your mother and I. You are simply getting out of hand. It is time we took sterner measures. Come with me," said Father, taking her hand.

"F-father! You're not going to *s-spank* me." He hadn't in *years!* "You're not going to!" pleaded Sarah.

"I am—and I will," said Father, leading the way to the woodshed.

And he did.

Afterward his arms held her close while she sobbed. She

told him then all about the lies and the naughtiness, right from the beginning.

"You need the Lord Jesus in your heart, lassie," he said.

"B-but I told B-brother Murchison that I w-was saved," she whispered.

"Another lie?" said Father, pressing his prickly cheek against hers.

Sarah nodded.

"Aren't you tired of running away from God? Wouldn't you like to be made clean and become His child?"

"Here? Now? Can I? Don't I even have to wait till the meeting?"

"Not at all! Here and now is the very best time and place."

Father sat on the chopping block, and he explained carefully how to be saved. Then both of them knelt and Sarah told the Lord Jesus that she wanted Him to clean her heart of all the sins, and to make her His girl. *He did.* Sarah knew it even before Father began to pray.

He was so happy he cried a bit too while he prayed, so Sarah couldn't help crying again in sympathy. But she was the happiest she had ever been in all her life, even if she'd have to be careful how she sat down for a while. She was pretty sore.

This was a strange day. Dinner at the Scotts' home was late because nobody had felt like eating while they were waiting for Father and her. They came into the kitchen together. Sarah's eyes felt puffy, but she smiled happily.

"I'm saved! Mother, I'm saved! I belong to Jesus now!"

Mother hugged her close, and for the second time that day Sarah heard her mother whisper, "I thank Thee, Lord Jesus!"

"And now you need a nap," said Mother after dinner.

"But—but I've got to go back to Aunt Jane's—"

Mother nodded. "But take a rest first. You need it."

Sarah slept and slept. Till five o'clock! Then for the second time that day she caught and bridled Captain. This time she rode slowly, and she rode only till the head of Miss Bolton's lane. She didn't want Linda to see her riding again—Linda, who loved riding so much.

The walk up the lane was a long, long walk. Sarah's heart was thumping and twice she almost turned back. Then she prayed in her heart, and she walked right up to the gate, along the walk, up the porch steps— She knocked on the door.

It opened. Aunt Jane stood there. "Well!" she said. "So it's you!"

As if—as if I'm a creepy, crawly something, thought Sarah. She swallowed.

"Aunt Jane—" But somehow the face before her didn't wear an Aunt Jane look today. Sarah began again.

"M-Miss Bolton, could I see Linda, please?"

"Could you give me a reason why I should allow it? A girl who could deliberately do what you did, Sarah Naomi Scott—"

"I'm very sorry. I came to say I was sorry. Please may I see Linda?"

Miss Bolton didn't seem to have heard. "If you could have seen her the way I found her! It took hours to calm her. And I can't have her upset again."

"I don't want to upset her. I—" Then she said it in a rush. "I asked Jesus into my heart today. I love Linda now. I want to tell her so. Please?"

"I'm afraid—I can't—risk it," said Aunt Jane.

Sarah searched Aunt Jane's face sadly. "Haven't you ever—done anything—that had to be forgiven?" she whispered, and she turned and ran down the walk.

She walked down the lane, slowly now. She had a nothing feeling, sort of like a burst balloon. Untying the halter rope was hard, because she couldn't see very clearly.

"Sarah? Little sister—" said a voice. Herbie stood there. He was covered with grease and dust and sweat. He looked *wonderful*. He had left his team of horses to come to her again. "In trouble again?"

Sarah sighed and nodded. Herbie had climbed to the topmost rail, just like last time. Sarah thought she better stand today. But she told him everything that happened today. He was so happy that she was saved. And he told her not to feel too bad about Miss Bolton. She had apologized for hurting Linda, so that was all that mattered. If God had forgotten that she ever did the wrong thing, she needn't go remembering it over and over.

"Does the Bible say that? About God forgetting?" said Sarah joyfully. "But—it happened this *morning*. How could He forget so quick?"

"Listen. I'll read it to you." He tugged a New Testament out of the bib pocket of his overalls. He read, "For I will be merciful to their unrighteousness, and their sins and their iniquities will I remember no more."

I will remember no more— That's forgetting. That really is!

Sarah said the words silently, getting happier and happier as she thought of them.

"Where does it say that?"

"Hebrews 8, verse 12. Can you remember?"

She nodded, looking into his dusty face lovingly. "I'm happy you're going to be my big brother."

"Are you?" But suddenly his face turned very serious. "Sarah, how is Kathleen?"

Sarah puckered up her forehead. "She's—different. Since the meetings started. She reads her Bible lots. And sometimes when I'm in bed she sits by the window, just looking out—"

"Over to my place?"

Sarah nodded. "And—and once she was crying a little— Herbie, is something the matter? You didn't quarrel, or anything?"

"No. Nothing like that. But—I believe God is calling me to become a minister. And I haven't talked to Kathleen about it."

"What if she doesn't want you to?"

"In that case, Sarah Naomi—" He stared soberly ahead again. "In that case I'll have to say yes to God anyway. And you see, even if it's all right with her, most likely we can't get married this year, the way we planned to."

"Why not?"

"I'll have to sell the farm—and the horses—and go to school—"

"Kathleen isn't going to like it," said Sarah decidedly.

"I was afraid of that."

"Shall I tell?"

"No. No, I'd rather do it."

He helped her mount Captain, and waved as she trotted away.

By the time Sarah got home supper was almost ready. Father and Stuart were unhitching in a hurry. Kathleen was helping Robbie feed the calves. Sarah rushed to feed the big and sassy goslings, and the lanky chickens. Everyone rushed through supper then, except maybe Robbie. He had to be reminded not to dawdle.

Kathleen was very silent while combing her hair. Sarah, already dressed for church, stood watching her make neat little earpuffs.

"Do something for me?" said Kathleen.

"What? Run away?"

"No, Sarah. I'd like you to—to *pray* for me. I—I need it. Will you?"

Sarah nodded quickly, and kissed Kathleen's neck, and slid toward the door. On the way to church no one spoke much. They were singing Brother Murchison's favorite song,

> "Blessed be the fountain of blood,
>   for a world of sinners revealed,
> Blessed be the dear Son of God,
>   only by His stripes we are healed . . .
> Though I've wandered far from the fold,
>   bringing to my heart pain and woe,
> Wash me in the blood of the Lamb,
>   and I shall be whiter than snow . . ."

The voices were rolling out so strong and happy. All of the Scotts were singing. All except Robbie.

CHAPTER 11

Aunt Jane

Bᴜᴛ ɴᴏᴛ ᴇᴠᴇʀʏᴛʜɪɴɢ is easy when you are a Christian. Sarah found that out the very first evening.

Robbie teased her when they were walking toward the church from the hitching post. "You'll have to testify—testify—testify—" he chanted in a whisper.

Almost every evening during the services Brother Hammond asked for testimonies. And that wouldn't be so bad. Sarah liked reciting poetry in public, or taking part in a play. Mostly when one of the boys and girls testified they said something like, "I'm glad Jesus is my Saviour now." Or, "I'm glad I'm saved."

But *they* hadn't told a lie, getting Brother Murchison to believe they were Christians when they weren't. She had.

Tonight her heart kept thumping, and she almost didn't speak up. *Tomorrow,* she thought. Maybe it would be easier tomorrow. Others were popping up here and there. She felt as if she was sitting on glue. Robbie kept looking sideways at her, teasing her with his eyes. Sarah chewed the insides of her cheeks nervously.

Brother Hammond had read the story about Gideon. Gideon was brave. He obeyed God even when other people thought he was foolish. Sarah's knees shook, but she got up.

"Well, Sarah?" said the minister, smiling.

"I—I" She licked her dry lips. Her heart was hammering on her tongue now. "I told a lie. I said I was saved. But I wasn't. But now I *am*. And I'm very glad."

"So are the angels in heaven, Sarah. Where and when did it happen?"

"Today—in—in the woodshed. Father helped me. He said I needn't wait till evening."

She sat down and she leaned her head against Father's arm.

"Many valuable lessons in life are learned in the woodshed," said Brother Hammond.

People laughed a little, and some cried a little. Father was wiping his eyes.

But Sarah was so happy!

Then a surprising thing happened. Stuart got up. He said he had been a Christian for a few years. But he hadn't ever had the courage to talk about it. Tonight his little sister had put him to shame. (*Was that a bad thing to do?* she wondered anxiously.) From now on he wanted to witness for the Lord whenever he had a chance.

Brother Murchison preached a real sermon. Sarah could almost hear Gideon's trumpets blaring, and hear the smashing pitchers, and see the torches flaring in the night. It was exciting. But the thing she would remember best later, happened at the close. When Brother Murchison asked if anybody wanted to be on the Lord's side, Robbie went forward. He didn't wait a single minute. He was brave as Gideon. Going home he was very quiet. But when Sarah squeezed his hand, he squeezed back, *hard*.

It had been a long and exciting day. This morning she rode to Aunt Ja— to Miss Bolton's. And then she hid in the secret place under the crab apple tree—and Father found her there, and took her to the woodshed—and when she came out she was a child of God! This afternoon she went back to Miss Bolton's—and they wouldn't let her in. And she met Herbie, and he told her about selling the farm to become a preacher.

Was he telling Kathleen about it now? She was going home with him in the runabout.

"They're there ahead of us," said Father.

And they were, waiting in the car at the garden gate. After a bit when the lamps were lit, Herbie came into the house with Kathleen. They looked serious, but their eyes had a shining look too.

So then Herbie told the news.

"God was calling both of us into His service. But we didn't know it of each other. Both of us became willing to give each other up—if it had to be—"

"But it doesn't have to be," said Kathleen, hugging Mother hard.

"And your farm?" said Father.

"I'm selling it."

"Is that necessary? Why not rent it to someone? There'd be an annual income while you are studying," said Father.

"No. I'll—I'll have to sell. Otherwise I might be tempted to go back to it when things get a bit rough."

"Perhaps you are right, perhaps you are right," said Father.

"It's sort of like Gideon and the grove," said Sarah. "Isn't it? Father, isn't it?"

Herbie answered for him. "It's exactly like that," he said.

Gideon had had to chop down the trees of the grove.

They weren't *wicked* trees. But people did wicked things there, worshiping idols. So the trees had to go. And being a farmer wasn't wicked. Look at Father! But God was calling Herbie to leave it.

Sometimes Sarah couldn't understand how he could do it. He liked farming so much. And he liked animals, liked working with them. He had built all the nifty new cupboards in the house for Kathleen and everything too. Now he and Kathleen would never live in the house at all. In the next weeks Kathleen never went to look at it again. Never once.

She was still sewing wedding things though. As soon as the threshing would be done in fall she and Herbie would be married, and they would drive away to Bible school. All the way to California!

The meetings were over. But in a way they would never be over. Things would never be the same. If Brother Murchison hadn't come, Herbie and Kathleen wouldn't be going so far away.

"What are we going to *do* without Kathleen?" Sarah asked her mother one day.

"We're going to miss her, I know. But let's give her to God joyfully. Sarah, if I could know that Keith was somewhere serving the Lord, even in a steaming jungle I'd be— I'd be happier than any words can express."

Keith. Sarah looked into Mother's face feeling sad for her. She guessed mothers and fathers never really forgot their sons even if they were gone for a long time. That was the way God had made them.

Mother did not speak of Keith again. "How about helping me to carry lunch to the field? You fill the water pail with good cold well water, and carry that."

This was harvesttime. Father was cutting the wheat with a binder. Round and round it went, its windmill arms turning, turning. Sarah loved the whirring sound. And the way the standing grain rippled and waved in the breeze. It looked like a huge golden lake, with the water rocking and dipping wherever you looked.

She loved the way the sheaves tumbled off the platform of the binder. And the way the stooks squatted here and there, like so many little Indian teepees. Stuart and Robbie did the stooking.

Robbie was getting pretty good at lifting up two heavy sheaves at a time, and knocking their heads together to set them upright in the stubble. Then you piled fourteen more sheaves all around. That was so if it rained the drops would go sliding down the slippery straw and not spoil the grain.

Sarah's shoes crunched across the stubble now. The water chug-chugged in the pail she carried. Its wire handle hurt her fingers some, but she loved lunching on the field.

Today Mother had packed salmon sandwiches, and new dill pickles, and cinnamon rolls still warm from the oven, and ladyfinger cookies with butterscotch icing. And hot creamy coffee made right in the pail.

The wind rustled through the wheat sheaves, as Sarah helped her mother unpack the things. The boys got to them first. Father, when he came, looked hot and worried. Something was wrong with the binder. He'd need some repairs from town—but he hardly had the time to go. Robbie was willing to go in his stead, just to get out of stooking! But Father said he couldn't be spared.

"What about you, Mother?"

"I'm afraid—" She shook her head. "I'm sorry, John. I'm afraid it's impossible."

"What about you, Princess?"

"To Blakely? *Alone?*"

"Why not? You know the way, and you often drive Wally."

Oh, *Wally.* For a moment she had had a picture of herself driving Hyacinthe proudly. But everyone seemed to think Hyacinthe was still too snuffy to be trusted in her hands. Father told Sarah exactly where to go in Blakely, and what to say when she got there. She could do it. He knew she could.

Wally never got excited. That was one good thing, in a way. Sarah's insides were quivering, and her hands shook a bit as she bridled and harnessed and hitched the sleepy old school horse. She didn't know—she couldn't know—that this was going to be a very adventurous ride.

The adventure began without her knowing it. She was going at a jog trot past Miss Bolton's place when she saw something flapping and flapping at a window. Not Linda's window. This was the dining room window. It looked almost like an arm waving. Sarah drove on. She was reciting Father's instructions over and over, so she'd not forget.

Go to Mr. Mason's hardware store, and ask for—

Suddenly she pulled the reins sharply. "Whoa!" she said, and she stared between Wally's ears.

She'd seen— What had she seen? Something like an arm waving—then just as she was passing it looked as if something flopped onto the arm— Could there be trouble at Aunt Jane's place?

There seemed to be two voices inside Sarah. Not exactly

arguing, but disagreeing. "Go back. They need you," said one. "Hurry to town and back, as fast as Wally can make it," said the other. This was what Father said just before she left home. And Father—well, you obeyed him, or else he'd know the reason why!

Sarah drove on. She clucked to Wally and shook out the reins, coaxing him into his fastest trot. In town for one horrible moment she thought she'd forgotten Father's message. But she hadn't. The hardware man laid the repairs on the floor of the buggy, and even turned Wally for her, so she could start back for home right away.

The horse thought he was tired. He wanted to slow to a walk.

"Aw, Wally! Only nine miles altogether! Come on now. Pick up your feet! We're going *home!*"

Maybe he heard. Maybe he understood. He began picking up speed. When they came close to Miss Bolton's place again the same inner voice began urging Sarah, *Turn in here. It needn't take long.*

She could see the binder from here. Father would be there, waiting for her. He would see her if she turned on the yard. But—she had to. Somehow she had to.

There was no one at the window now. Sarah urged Wally to a fast run. She pulled up in front of the gate, and quickly she scrambled down to tie the halter rope. Then she went running up the walk.

She knocked—and waited—and knocked again. Her heart was hammering. But she heard *something.*

"Anybody *home?*" she called, and knocked again.

The same sound came—a groan. And now someone was calling, "Oh, please come. Oh, somebody, please come!"

Sarah tried the knob. It turned. The door wasn't locked.

The next minute she was blinking in the little dark entry.

"Hello?" she said timidly.

"Oh!" said a voice. "Oh, you've *come!*"

Sarah moved into the dining room. The first thing she saw was Linda huddled on the floor in the doorway that led to her room. And beside her lay Aunt Jane. Her eyes were closed, but she was groaning softly. She looked dreadful.

"She fell! Down the stairs!" Linda's teeth were chattering as if she was cold. "And she's been lying there, and *lying* there— And I couldn't reach the phone—"

The phone! Sarah ran to the kitchen. She cranked the handle, two longs, two shorts. The home number. Her heart was thumping.

"Don't cry, Linda," she called over her shoulder. "Please, don't cry. It's going to be all right. Oh, why doesn't Mother answer?"

She cranked the handle again and again. Mother must be outside, probably hoeing the garden.

Please, Lord Jesus, let her hear—

"Say! Anything *wrong?*" shouted a voice into the receiver.

That was Mrs. Heathe answering. They were on the same party line.

"Mrs. Heathe? This is Sarah Scott. And I'm at Aunt Jane's place—Jane Bolton's—and she's had an accident. Could you please—"

And then she heard her mother say, "Hello? Hello?"

Now everything was going to be all right. Everything was in good hands.

But Sarah still had to wait for help to come. Every min-

ute crawled by, slow as a snail. Sarah crouched on the floor beside Aunt Jane and Linda, and the two girls talked in whispers.

"How did it happen?"

"Well, she was busy all morning—you know the way she does. Housecleaning upstairs, washing windows and walls. And I guess she stumbled, or something—"

"Probably slipped on something. Soap, or something—"

"Probably. I heard her fall, and I was terribly frightened. She just *lay* there. And she began moaning. And I was sitting on my chair, so first I had to get to the floor. And then I got to the window—and I saw you passing—and I waved—but you just kept going—"

Sarah felt awful about that, but she slipped her arm around Linda's shoulder and patted it.

"Don't, Linda. Don't think about that now. Mother will be here soon."

It was a sad time. But—they were *friends!* Sarah felt it—and she thought that Linda must feel it too.

Mother came—and the doctor from Paxton. And the ambulance. The Heathes came first, bringing not only Mother but Father as well. After Aunt Jane had gone with the ambulance, Mother quickly packed some of Linda's things, and Father picked the girl up to carry her out to the car.

"But where am I *going?* I have no place to stay now."

"There'll be room in our home for you as long as you need it, Linda," Sarah heard Father say as he got into the car, still holding her carefully.

Sarah watched them go. Then, sighing a bit, she untied Wally and turned him and the buggy, and climbed in.

"Giddap!" she said, slapping the reins smartly down on his back.

CHAPTER 12

A Dream Come True

B<small>Y THE TIME</small> Sarah reached home, Linda was asleep on the living room couch. She never awoke at all until next morning. Mother said the poor child must have been completely exhausted by the long anxious vigil beside Aunt Jane after the accident.

It seemed strange to think that Linda was in this house. Linda Bolton! The Scott family kept their voices down at the supper table so as not to disturb her.

Mother and Father had been in town with the Heathes. The doctor said Aunt Jane's hip was broken, and she'd suffered a concussion too. She still wasn't conscious. It might be a long, long time before she could come back home again.

"And we keep Linda here? Oh, let's," said Sarah.

"That's for Mother to say," answered Father. "Most of the work is certain to fall on her."

"I'm not so sure about that. Sarah is likely to have to run the errands. It won't be easy. If we keep Linda until her father can make a new home for her—or until Aunt Jane is well once more—and I believe we ought to— *If* we do, it will be a family responsibility. And there'll be no backing out. Do you really want her here, Sarah?"

"Oh, yes, yes, yes!"

"Let's not make any long-term plans. For now our home is hers—if she wants it. Let's wait to see how it works out," suggested Father.

So that was the way it was.

Next morning Sarah could hardly wait till Linda woke. Even then she had to wait. Kathleen gave the patient a bath and freshened her up for the day. Then Sarah pushed the door open carefully and brought in Linda's breakfast tray. She had tucked a cluster of wood anemones beside the glass of milk, and she thought the tray looked lovely.

When she had set it down her eyes sought Linda's half fearfully though. Her meetings with Linda hadn't been exactly happy ones so far.

"Mmmm, I'm hungry," said Linda. "And you're all so *good* to me."

Sarah felt herself getting red. "Not always," she said in a sorry voice.

"Well! You're not going to talk about *that,* are you? Then I'd have to think about the way I behaved to you when you came to see me that first day. In June, was it—or May—"

"May twenty-fifth," said Sarah.

"You remembered! That's funny. Well, anyway, let's just forget, huh?"

"Let's," agreed Sarah, relieved.

She held out her sturdy brown hand and Linda slipped her thin white one inside it. Such a frail hand.

Linda giggled. "This is our promise that we'll always remember to forget," she said. And then she settled down to enjoy her breakfast.

Sarah sat on the floor beside the couch, talking about all the things that happen on a farm in summer.

"I wish I could see it," sighed Linda.

Sarah had an idea. But—it might not work.

"Do your legs hurt?" she said anxiously.

"Not anymore. They did at first, dreadfully. Now they're just sort of numb and useless."

They looked it. Like Samanatha's rag-doll legs, dangly and thin.

"Well, does your back hurt if it gets jiggled about a bit?"

"N-no. I don't think so. I never get a chance to find out. Sarah, you have an idea! What is it?"

"Well, maybe you'll think it silly—or—or—*crude*—"

"Sarah Naomi Scott! You've forgotten to forget already!"

Sarah felt herself getting pink. "No, but *really*," she said. "Listen. We have a wheelbarrow, and Father or Stuart could carry you outside, easy as easy. And we could have blankets to make it nice and soft, and I could wheel you around to see the garden and the whole yard."

"And the creek? I'd love to see a creek. It's been so *long* since I've been near running water. Aunt Jane said she bought the car so we could go places together, but somehow we never did. She always had so many things to do."

Sarah was a bit doubtful about wheeling Linda down to the creek. The slope was so steep in places, and bumpy besides.

"We'll see," she said, just as Mother might have. Maybe Father could take the time to wheel her down sometime.

He did carry her out, after Sarah had swept the barrow clean, and Mother had padded the inside with wool comforters and pillows.

"But we'll need to dress you warmly," remarked Mother.

"Today?" said Sarah astonished. "But, Mother, it's hot outside!"

"For you perhaps. Look at Linda. She's shaking now."

Mostly that was from the excitement of going out after months and months of being cooped up indoors. The thin arm she slid around Father's neck was shaking. And her breath came in shivery gusts. But her blue eyes shone with happiness and interest.

Where the ground was level, Sarah's job was fairly easy. She and Linda were in no hurry. They rested every little while so Linda could pat Spencer again. He licked her hand gently, and never pounced on her the way he did Sarah. And he paced slowly beside them when Sarah took up the handles again. Ginger sat curled up in Linda's lap, blinking and purring.

They trundled down the garden walk. (But Sarah didn't show Linda her most secret place. Not yet. Someday maybe.) Sarah pulled two carrots, and scrubbed them with the green leaves, and they crunched them. Then Sarah spied a ripe tomato on the vine. The first one. She raced indoors to ask permission—and raced out again to pick it and share it with Linda. Mmmmm— Then they picked handfuls of green peas and ate them.

It was time then to take a look into the barns and granaries and the pigpen. Just to peer inside. Sarah couldn't wheel over the sills. Besides, she guessed that Linda might think them too *smelly*. (But little piggies are the cutest things.) Linda never once used the word. She looked as if she wasn't even *thinking* it. Beauty and Daisy's colts were poking their heads through the bars of the gate. Linda stroked their velvety noses. She had tears in her eyes, though she tried to hide them. Sarah looked around quickly for a way to divert Linda.

"Are you tired? If not I'll show you something funny," she said.

And she called out, "Peelee, peelee, peelee—"

You should have seen the geese! They were about all grown up now. They were not fenced in or anything. They could go swimming any old time of the day. But when they heard Sarah's call they lined up, all thirty-three of them, and they waddled behind her, one foot up, one foot down, all the way to the creek!

Laughing, Sarah came racing back up the hill then. But Linda— Linda had a look on her face that said, *And I'll never be able to run again!*

Sarah came to a sudden stop. "I wasn't thinking, Linda. I'm s-sorry—"

"Don't be." Her thin hands clutched Sarah's arm and shook it a bit. "Don't ever be. It won't do *my* legs any good if you don't use yours."

And that was true. But all the same it was a relief to Sarah that minute to hear her mother calling from the porch, "Time for Linda to take a rest now."

Later, that afternoon, Kathleen took Linda and the wheelbarrow out to the meadow to round up the cows. That was fun. Sarah ran alongside, picking flowers and bringing them to Linda. Spencer did most of the real work. Linda had never seen cows so close before. Imagine! She had pink cheeks when they got back to the house. And at suppertime she sat at the table in an armchair, eating with everyone else. She said she'd had a marvelous day.

"I don't mean I'm not sorry for Aunt Jane—"

"We understand. And there's no need to feel guilty. It wouldn't help her. What we can do for your aunt is to pray."

"I—I suppose so," said Linda uncertainly.

Maybe Linda didn't know about prayer. Maybe no one had ever taught her. Then maybe one reason why God allowed the accident to happen was so that Linda would get to hear about Jesus—

Shortly after supper the telephone rang. Two longs, two shorts. The Scott ring. When Mother answered, she found that Aunt Jane's nurse was calling. The patient was conscious part of the time now, but very restless. And she kept calling for Sarah Scott.

"You're sure she didn't say Sheila Scott?" Sarah heard her mother say. Then she stood listening. "Very well. We'll try to bring her in," said Mother, and she hung up the receiver.

"Linda?" said Sarah who had heard only one side of the conversation.

Mother shook her head. "It seems that Aunt Jane has been asking for you, Sarah."

Sarah didn't at all like the idea, but both Father and Mother thought she ought to go. And later Sarah was glad. On the way to Paxton Mother spoke of many things, remembering how it was when she and Aunt Jane were best friends.

Herbie started it. He was taking them in, and he asked questions. Once when *Sarah* did, Mother wouldn't answer! Now she began remembering aloud—

"Aunt Jane's mother died when she was little, and her father spoiled her a bit. She always had her own way. Some people called her cold and proud. But she was never anything but generous and warmhearted to me."

"But what happened to change that, Mrs. Scott? Whose fault was it?"

"Who knows? Well, God does, I'm sure. Someone started an idle rumor. It grew and grew the way gossip does. Someone told Jane that *I* had begun it. And I'll admit that circumstantial evidence— Do you know what that means, Sarah?"

"I—I *think* so—sorta."

"Well, circumstantial evidence seemed to prove that I had said the things I was accused of saying. My denial only made the situation worse." Just thinking and talking about it made Mother look sad—almost the way she looked whenever she mentioned Keith. Sarah squeezed her hand, and they were quiet the rest of the way.

It's a scarey thing, in a way, to walk into a hospital for the first time. Aunt Jane's doctor met them in the hall. His eyebrows shot up when he saw Sarah. They seemed to say, *Is this Sarah Naomi Scott? What's so important about her? I expected a grown-up.*

Aloud he said, "This way, please. If she asks questions, answer briefly and reassuringly. Don't chatter. We musn't tire out patient, you know."

Sarah had never felt less like chattering in all her life. The doctor had led them into a little room where Aunt Jane lay. Such a wrinkled face! White, still, with deep sunken eyes— This couldn't be Aunt Jane!

The eyes opened. She saw Mother first.

"Sheila-Sheila—" The eyes closed, and tears were slipping down her cheekbones. Mother stooped over to kiss her forehead.

Aunt Jane said slowly, "The question— Sarah asked a question— Couldn't forget— She said—she said—'H-have you never— Never done anything—that needs—for—forgiveness?' Couldn't forget the question— Tell Sarah Naomi—"

Then she fell asleep!

"Better go now," whispered the doctor.

Sarah cried a bit on the way home. Mother let her. Sarah wondered, *Will Mother and Aunt Jane be real friends again now?* And she remembered something—

"Mother, 'way back in spring you said that God had shown you a way to prove to Aunt Jane that you still loved her. How, Mother?"

"Do you happen to remember the kind of chinaware she had on the tray on the day Linda arrived?"

That was a funny question. But Sarah thought hard. It was pretty china, special china—

"A rose pattern, I think, with fancy crinkly edges, all in gold. Why, Mother?"

"Aunt Jane's favorite pattern. I used to buy the pieces for her, one at a time, when we were young girls. Every Christmas and Easter and birthday, all these years, I mailed another piece, enclosing no name or note."

Sarah thought that was a funny thing to do. She wondered how Aunt Jane felt when she unwrapped the parcels and parcels that kept coming. Each one said, *I still love you, Jane Bolton.* And she maybe pretending she didn't know who sent it!

Mother said that was just the way people behaved toward God when He kept sending His love tokens—sunshine, food, clothing and good health— Sarah thought of her two good strong legs. She didn't think she had ever thanked God for them! Not once.

Poor Linda, with her rag-doll legs— But all the Scotts were praying that God would heal her. He could! Wouldn't

it be *splendid* if she and Linda could go riding and climbing trees and running together!

By the following Saturday Aunt Jane was a lot better in her mind, even if her broken hip would take a long while to heal. She and Mother were friends again. It took just a few words to clear away the big mountain of misunderstanding and bitterness. Best of all, Aunt Jane had come back to God! It was like the Bible story of the man who said, "I will arise and go to my father—" And the father was waiting. All those years and years God must have been waiting for Aunt Jane too.

By Saturday Father had used the big scoop—called a Fresno—with Prince and Captain hitched to it, to smooth the slope to the creek. Most of the afternoons now, for almost *all* afternoon, Sarah took Linda down the gentle slope to play. They played under the rustling trees. They made doll clothes—and talked. They read books together—and they talked. They built little houses and forts of sticks and stones—and they talked. They never got done! The creek chattered too. But Spencer mostly lay at Linda's feet. He had deserted Robbie of late. He seemed to think he had to guard Linda.

"He's a gentleman," said Linda. "All the people at your house are gentlemen. And ladies," she added hastily. They laughed. "You know what I mean," said Linda.

"Well, this lady has to go and polish a lot of shoes," said Sarah. She got to her feet and stretched. "Ooooh! I'd almost forgotten. It's *Saturday!*"

"What's so special about Saturday?" said Linda.

"You'll see."

Pushing the wheelbarrow uphill was hopeless for Sarah. For this job she had a rope that went around her neck and under her arms and fastened to the handles of the barrow. "Ready? Hold tight," said the human pony, beginning the slow climb.

There was the usual Saturday rush to eat supper and wash dishes and to gather around the organ. But to Sarah everything seemed different. Linda was there!

She didn't sing along with them. Maybe she hardly knew any of the songs. But she sat propped on the couch, and her eyes grew big and shiny as Stuart sang out,

"Oh, come, come, come come. . . ."

Come to the church in the wildwood! Tomorrow was Sunday.

Kathleen would be staying at home with Linda. But soon, perhaps, Linda would be able to go to church with them. She was getting stronger every day, she said. She was really getting brown! Best of all, she was learning a bit more about the Bible and about the Saviour every day.

They were friends—just as Sarah had hoped they would be, long and long ago.

Maybe soon Linda would discover that the best friend of all was Jesus.

Sometimes Sarah thought she could hardly wait!